She was seeing things

Lexy blinked. Familiar sapphire blue eyes stared back at her. He automatically shoved that stubborn lock of light brown hair off his forehead, the same way she remembered.

"Matthew?" she whispered.

His lips curved in a tentative smile. "Hi, Allessandra."

"No one calls me that anymore." The shock of finding him at her door continued to seep in, and her knees were getting all rubbery and useless.

He slapped a hand against the door when she would have closed it. "We have a problem."

She froze. He looked so serious all of a sudden. Serious enough to make her heart start to pound, to make her head grow light. He couldn't possibly know. He couldn't.

He frowned, then studied her for a long, disconcerting moment.

"We're still married."

Dear Reader,

As many times as people have asked me how I come up with ideas for my books, you'd think I wouldn't still get dumbfounded and have to flounder for an answer. But I do. Until I married my practical, reality-based husband, I figured everyone had strange characters and situations hopping around in their heads. Wrong. I guess the fact that I do makes me a writer.

In *Overnight Father*, Matthew sunk his hooks into me first. How would a man who was about to be married react if he found out his first marriage had not been annulled as he had believed for seven years? What would happen if he were a prominent attorney who couldn't afford a scandal?

Figuring out just who could give him a run for his money turned out to be even more interesting. And fun. Lexy fit the bill perfectly—complete with her offbeat family members. Who, I must point out, have no characteristics of my own, er, "interesting" family. Especially since my mother will likely read this.

I hope you enjoy reading about Matthew and Lexy's journey as much as I enjoyed prodding it along.

Thanks to all my readers for making my dream possible. May all yours come true, too.

Debbi Rawlins

Overnight
Father

DEBBI RAWLINS

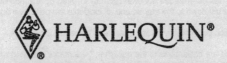

TORONTO • NEW YORK • LONDON
AMSTERDAM • PARIS • SYDNEY • HAMBURG
STOCKHOLM • ATHENS • TOKYO • MILAN • MADRID
PRAGUE • WARSAW • BUDAPEST • AUCKLAND

ISBN 0-373-16790-3

OVERNIGHT FATHER

ABOUT THE AUTHOR

Debbi Rawlins currently lives with her husband and dog in Durham, North Carolina. A native of Hawaii, she married on Maui and has since lived in Cincinnati, Chicago, Tulsa, Houston and Detroit. One of her favorite things about living on the mainland is snow. She can't get enough of it. Unfortunately, the milder Durham climate doesn't always cooperate.

When Debbi isn't busy at the computer, she is lost between the pages of a book or headed for the airport and parts unknown.

Books by Debbi Rawlins

HARLEQUIN AMERICAN ROMANCE

LOVE AND LAUGHTER

For Tashya Wilson. Thanks for catching the ball, juggling a few more and running with them all. You've done a terrific job. Your patience and attention to detail have helped make me a better writer. Thank you.

Chapter One

"Prominent Divorce Attorney Arrested For Bigamy. I can see the headlines now."

Matthew Monroe cringed at his friend's teasing words. This couldn't be happening. Not now. Not to him. He stared down at the certificate for a marriage that should have been annulled seven years ago. He was supposed to marry his boss's daughter in six weeks. "Don't forget who got me into this mess, pal."

"Oh, no, you're not gonna pin this on me," Brad said, holding his hands up. "I did you a favor by introducing you to Lexy. You wouldn't have had enough money to get through law school if it hadn't been for her." Brad frowned. "Your ex-wife." Then he grinned, his green eyes crinkling with amusement. "But I guess she isn't your ex yet."

Matt darted a nervous glance at his closed office door. "I don't want to talk about this here," he said, shoving the marriage certificate back into the worn, faded envelope. "How about we meet at Sandalwood's for a drink after work? A martini sounds damn good."

Instead of getting up, Brad slumped more comfortably in his chair and peered at Matt over steepled fingers. "You're going to have to tell Amanda."

"The hell I will." Matt snorted at the absurdity of his friend's suggestion. "What we did was illegal. You know what a temper Amanda has. All she has to do is go running to Daddy and blow the whistle on me. And there goes my partnership."

Brad stared at him in silence, his eyebrows dipping in a concerned frown. Matt let his gaze drop to the frayed corner of the envelope. No way was he getting into another useless discussion about the fallacy of his upcoming marriage. Marrying Amanda made sense for both of them.

He shifted against the uncomfortable silence. His friend's penetrating stare seemed to summon the past like a magician pulling a rabbit out of a hat. Marriage to Lexy had been necessary. They were young. He needed money. She needed a Green Card. This was totally different.

Lexy.

He'd thought about her over the years. It wasn't hard to picture her now, the long, dark hair, eyes as brown and rich as fine Belgian chocolate, the slim curves...she'd been something to look at, all right.

And sweet. Too sweet. A real dreamer. He hoped she'd found the white picket fence she wanted.

He shoved the envelope into his middle desk drawer and flipped through his phone directory. "Get out, Brad. I have work to do."

The same stern tone that normally sent law clerks scurrying to do Matt's bidding was lost on his best friend of eleven years. Brad yawned and stretched his arms over his head. When he was finished, he said, "You want me to talk to Lexy?"

Matt set aside the directory, leaned back in his chair and idly stroked the fine black leather. The thought hadn't occurred to him. Although it held merit. He didn't particularly want to see her again. Not after that last night. "I don't know where she is. She could have moved out of the state for all I know."

Brad shrugged. "Unless she's moved back to Hungary, it shouldn't be hard to find her. I doubt she's done that."

Exhaling, Matt nodded his agreement. Maybe this matter could go away quietly. "I'd owe you one."

His friend straightened, his lips curving. "No problem. Pretty thing like her probably has a string of men lined up. I'd expect she'd want to get this straightened out, too, so I'd be doing her a favor." His grin broadened. "No telling how grateful she'll be."

The cocky smile that normally made Matt chuckle angered him. They were talking about Lexy here. Sweet, soft-spoken, vulnerable Lexy. Not one of Brad's bimbo girlfriends.

Matt cleared his throat. Emotion had no place in business. And this, essentially, was business. "Look, I don't want to get you involved—"

"Hey, what are friends for?" Brad stood, looking a little more animated. He had that thrill-of-the-chase look Matt recognized well. As ambitious as Matt was, Brad was equally laid-back. Except when it came to the ladies. "I'll get right on it. I bet I find her before happy hour at Sandalwood's."

"I'll handle this, Brad. You have that big case coming up next week and—"

"Consider the matter closed." Brad stopped at the door to waggle his eyebrows and dramatically adjust the lapels of his Armani suit. "Old Brad will take care of everything."

The swell of irritation nearly sent Matt flying out of his chair. In his best lawyer's voice, he calmly said, "I'll handle this myself."

The total absence of expression on his friend's face confused him. Brad wasn't one to hide his feelings. But he just stood there, watching, waiting.

But there was nothing else to say. Lexy was off limits to the likes of Brad. Case closed. Matt had hurt her enough.

LEXY STARTED A SECOND stack of bills and purposely placed them near the chip on the right corner of the narrow yellow Formica counter. That way she knew she'd have enough room to lay out the other bills that would have to wait until next payday. Or the payday after that.

One good thing about having two jobs, she figured, was that she also had two paydays. Even though her combined income didn't amount to much, they never went without milk as a result.

Staring at the bottom total of the electric bill, she shook her head. She'd turned the air conditioner up, started using the oven only once a week. How had the amount climbed?

She made a notation to pay this one in full. Last month she'd paid only half. This time it was the water company's turn to wait for some of their money. She might be poor, more than a little humiliated, but she was at least fair.

She sighed and took another sip of water. She hated living this way. Her parents would be mortified if they knew. They'd sent her to this country for a better life.

But her parents were another problem. One she couldn't think about right now. It was too depressing, and she had finals to study for. She wouldn't get out of this financial hole until she finished her degree and got a real job. And she was so close...

The doorbell buzzed, startling her, annoying her. She was counting on a rare, peaceful afternoon to study. Tempted to not answer, she gave in and plodded to the door. Her caller could be here about Tasha. But if it was a solicitor, she wasn't going to be nice.

She opened the door, and time stopped.

She was seeing things. Too many late nights working the dinner shift. Too much studying into the wee hours. And now she was hallucinating. Seeing ghosts from her past.

No...demons.

Lexy blinked. Familiar sapphire-blue eyes stared back at her. He automatically shoved that stubborn lock of light-brown hair off his forehead, the same way she remembered. Only, his shoulders seemed broader now.

"Matthew?" she whispered.

His lips curved in a tentative smile. That was new, too. Matthew was always very sure of himself. "Hi, Alessandra."

"No one calls me that anymore." The shock of finding him at her door continued to seep in, and her knees were getting all rubbery and useless. She stiffened. "What do you want, Matthew?"

His smile slipped and he stared at her with an odd expression on his face. "I would have called first, but Directory said you don't have a phone."

She blinked again. Last month things had finally

gotten too tight to warrant the small luxury. "Phones are an intrusion, and I'm a busy person."

Her sudden boldness took her by surprise. In the old days she would never have dreamed of being abrupt with Matthew. She straightened, sort of liking the new her.

He nodded absently, his gaze fastened to her face. "Of course, I'll get to the point." He frowned. "What happened to your accent?"

His question flooded her with pride. She'd worked hard at her English. She shrugged. "I still have one."

"Yeah, but not much," he said, suddenly studying her so hard it made her want to squirm. "And your hair." He started to reach out a hand, then stopped himself. "When did you cut it?"

She touched the ends of her shoulder-length hair and winced when she realized she'd barely run a brush through it since this morning. And makeup. She hadn't bothered today. Oh, heaven help her, she must look awful.

Tugging self-consciously at her ratty white T-shirt, she backed up a step. Matthew took one forward, and she stopped, her other hand gripping the doorknob so hard she felt it give a little. She'd have to replace that screw one of these days.

"We don't have anything to say to each other, Matthew." He couldn't come in. The apartment was possibly a bigger mess than she was.

"Wait." He slapped a hand against the door when she would have closed it. "We have a problem."

She laughed without humor. That was an understatement. "Nothing mutual, I'm sure."

"I'm afraid so."

She froze. He looked so serious all of a sudden.

Serious enough to make her heart start to pound, to make her head grow light. He couldn't possibly know. He couldn't.

The full impact of Matthew showing up at her door after all these years gripped her like a noose around her neck. He had to leave. Now. He had no claims here.

"I'll call the police if I have to," she said, and realized how foolish she sounded when he reared his head back in open astonishment. She took a deep breath. "What is it, Matthew?"

He narrowed his eyes, his gaze sweeping past her, over her shoulder, into her small, shabby kitchen. "Can we talk inside?"

"No."

His quick frown ended with a sigh. "What I have to discuss is a little touchy, and I doubt you want your neighbors eavesdropping."

Oh, God, this was her worst nightmare. But how could he have found out? And why, after all these years, would he care? She tried to swallow back the fear that had lodged like a stubborn wad of bubble gum in her throat, but there was no easy answer for why Matthew was here. She was in trouble. She'd read about him in the newspaper once. He was rich, powerful now. And he was the most determined, single-minded man she'd ever met. She remembered that all too well. Their last night together was reminder enough.

Maybe she shouldn't antagonize him. Maybe if she were a little nicer. Maybe if...

"Lexy, are you going to let me in?" Matthew ducked his head to meet her gaze and smiled.

She took an extra-deep breath, trying to stabilize her

breathing. It didn't work. It couldn't. Matt was looking at her with those beautiful blue eyes of his, and she'd reverted to the same shy nineteen-year-old whose starry-eyed dreams wished for the impossible.

"Lexy?"

She briefly closed her eyes to clear her head, then stepped farther back without saying another word and watched him casually eye her dingy furnishings as he advanced into her minuscule living room.

She couldn't imagine what he was thinking. Both the pink plaid couch and the leaning walnut side table had been purchased from a thrift shop. She'd picked up the pale green recliner at a yard sale. And she wouldn't even have the small fifteen-year-old TV if it weren't for her kindhearted neighbor.

None of the items reflected her taste. Only her empty bank account.

"Have a seat," she said, and when he hesitated, she added, "It's clean."

Color seeped into his tanned complexion, and he turned wordlessly to settle himself on the pink couch. Even as it shamed her to have caused his discomfort, his reaction fascinated her, too. This wasn't the brash young law student she remembered. The one who'd claimed he'd someday set the world of law on its ear. The same man who'd informed her that a family would only weigh him down.

"So, Matthew, what is it you think I can help you with?" she asked, pleased with the steadiness of her voice. However, she had to clasp her hands together to keep from shaking.

"Have you lived here long?" he asked, his tone pleasant, conversational, and she wanted to hit him.

"About four years."

"Imagine us still living in the same city and not ever running into each other."

"I only go to the country club on Thursdays," she said blandly.

Annoyance replaced his smile. "Am I supposed to apologize because we don't run in the same circles?"

Shame found her again and she looked away. She was happy for his success. No doubt he'd worked hard. He deserved it. "Look, I'm sorry. I—" She broke off and sank into the lumpy recliner. "I didn't mean—"

"Forget it." He tugged at his tie, and for a moment looked as uncomfortable as Lexy felt. "You look good."

That startled a laugh out of her.

"What?" His surprise seemed genuine as a smile slowly spread across his face, and he once again looked like the handsome young law student she'd foolishly fallen in love with seven years ago. "What's so funny, Lexy?"

She stared back at him, enjoying the way his left cheek grooved when he grinned, the sparkling blue of his eyes. Until a surge of anger mentally shook her. Nothing was funny.

Absolutely nothing.

She sobered, recalling the callous way he'd disappeared. "You haven't told me why you're here."

At her abrupt change in mood, he frowned, then studied her for a long, disconcerting moment. "We're still married."

If he'd intended to shock her again, he'd done a heck of a job. She slumped against the recliner back, barely feeling the loose spring that poked her hip.

"But you were going to handle that." She waved a

hand, irritated that she couldn't find the proper English word. "That, that legal thing—" She exhaled in frustration. This only happened when she got upset. Normally, her English was nearly perfect.

"Annulment," he offered.

"So why didn't you do that?"

"I thought I had."

"Oh, some big-shot lawyer you are." Her hand flapped through the air, the gesture so much like something her flamboyant mother would make that it gave Lexy pause.

"So I made one little mistake." Temper flared in his eyes. "I'm not any happier about this than you are."

"How do you know whether I'm happy? You don't know anything about me," she said, her voice rising, making her sound like her mother, too. And worse, her accent had become more pronounced.

One side of Matthew's mouth started to curve. "You sound like your old self."

She let out a low shriek. "No, I don't. I am not the same person you knew, Matthew. I will never be that—that naive young child again."

He blinked, and something that looked like guilt cast a brief shadow across his face. "We were both young," he said quietly.

She didn't want to have this conversation with him. No sense in opening old wounds. Besides, she couldn't really blame him. He'd been perfectly honest about what he'd wanted from her...and didn't want. Sleeping with him that last night had been her choice. And given the chance, she would change nothing.

Lexy tried to smile. She actually had a lot to be happy about. This problem was very mild compared to what she'd imagined. She just had to get rid of him before Tasha came home, then life would be back to normal.

"Okay," she said, and tried not to notice how attractive she found him. He'd always had great hands, but they looked stronger now, more capable. They'd done wonderful things to her breasts. Abruptly, she lifted her gaze to his face. "You need me to sign something?"

He nodded, a slight frown creasing his forehead. Age agreed with him. He looked more rugged, not so boyish. "You aren't married, are you? To someone else?"

"No."

"Have you ever been?"

She shook her head.

"I didn't think so."

At the confident look on his face, irritation singed her. Did he not think she would make a fine wife? She glared at him. "Why?"

He shrugged. "You kept the name Monroe. That surprised me. Made you easy to find, though."

"Oh."

"Since neither of us have married since our so-called annulment, this problem shouldn't be too hard to rectify."

The fact that he hadn't married again should have meant nothing to her but it did. She glanced at his hands and smiled. "Whenever you have the paperwork ready I'll come by and sign it."

"I'm having the documents drawn up now." He tugged at his tie. "We'll have to settle this right away."

She pursed her lips. Something else was bothering him.

"Will you be available tomorrow?" he asked.

She shook her head. "I have two finals."

His eyebrows rose. "As in exams?"

Lexy straightened. Why couldn't she learn that a simple no was sufficient? He didn't need to know anything personal about her. "Yes."

"You're still in school?"

She sighed. "Yes. How about next week?"

Frowning, Matthew stared absently at her. After a long pause, he said, "I need this settled immediately."

"Okay." She mentally flipped through her calendar. The restaurant had her scheduled every night for the next week. Studying would ease up, but she had the administrative offices to clean before the end of school break. She'd do that first thing each morning. Then, of course, there were Tasha's ballet lessons, laundry that could no longer wait, grocery shopping, the cookies she'd promised to bake...

"Lexy?" He waved a hand in front of her face. "You still with me?"

"I'm not the one who left, Matthew."

As soon as the words were out of her mouth, she wanted to crawl between the warped kitchen floorboards and disappear forever. How could she have said such a thing? She tried to swallow, but her throat no longer worked.

Chancing a fleeting look at Matthew's displeased face, she pushed to her feet. "I'm sorry I didn't offer you something to drink," she said. Too late, she realized she didn't have anything to offer. Maybe a little milk, but that was it. Without waiting for his answer, she grabbed the glass of water she'd left on the counter and took a large gulp.

The liquid soothed her acid tongue and glided down her parched throat. She wasn't going to apologize. She wasn't the one who'd suddenly shown up after seven years without a word. "Did you want something?" she asked.

"A little slack?"

"How about some water?"

His lips curved in a wry smile. "This doesn't have to be difficult, Lexy. And for what it's worth, I am sorry about what happened between us."

"Nothing happened, Matthew." The irony of that truth was like a slap of common sense. "How does Saturday sound?"

His gaze roamed her face, briefly touched her breasts, and the way his eyes suddenly darkened, she knew he was remembering that last night, too.

She turned away to get more water. Not because she wanted it but because her traitorous body was getting all tight and hot from the look he'd given her.

"Maybe I will take some of that water," he said, and she stifled the sudden smile that tugged at her lips.

She got a jelly glass out of the cupboard and filled it with tap water. No doubt he was used to some fancy mineral stuff. Too bad. "Here you go."

"Thanks." He crossed the small room and accepted the glass, making no move to avert his eyes. His gaze met hers squarely. "I'm getting married."

Taken aback by the news, she clutched the side of the counter for support. She wasn't supposed to care. But he'd said he'd never marry, that he wanted a career, not a family.

She forced a smile, pushed away from the counter and shouldered past him. "Congratulations. When?"

"Next month."

"I see." She carried her water to the recliner and sank into the lumpy green upholstery. "So you need to make our marriage go away."

He jerked a little at her tone. Staring at the back of his head, she winced, too. She hadn't meant to sound bitter. She was happy for him. Really. As her young American co-worker would say, good riddance.

"Look, I'll squeeze some time out tomorrow," she said, hoping her boss would give her an hour or two off before the dinner rush. "But it will have to be before five."

Matthew slowly turned away from the open kitchen and faced her. He made no move to sit down. His expression pensive, he asked, "Why are you still in school? You were a sophomore when we—"

"I know." She shrugged. "Things came up."

"Money problems?"

She shifted, her pride tweaked. He'd handed her a great opening. She could be nasty and remind him that he'd taken most of her savings in exchange for their fake marriage. But she kept her mouth shut and shrugged. "Among other things."

He turned to the window and squinted out at the gray May sky, his forehead furrowed as if he were deep in thought. She glanced at the small antique clock, one of the few possessions she'd brought from Hungary. Tasha would be home in forty minutes. He needed to leave.

"I have an idea," he said.

She stood in order to hurry him along.

"I'm giving you back the money you paid me."

"What?" She nearly flipped over her glass. "We had a deal. I don't want your charity now, Matthew."

"This isn't charity. I'm just trying to make things right."

He wanted to pay her off, soothe his conscience. That stung. She pushed past him toward the door. "Out, before I really get mad."

The doorknob wouldn't cooperate. She jiggled it, but it had finally gotten so loose, it wouldn't open. Great.

"Come on, Lexy, don't let your temper stand in the way of reason. Let me explain. This isn't—"

She skewered him with a dirty look and hit the knob with the heel of her hand. "My temper is none of your business, Matthew. *I* am none of your business."

"Are you going to let me explain?"

"No."

He closed the distance between them, and she held her breath when his shoulder brushed her arm and his chin grazed the top of her head. Hesitantly, she gazed up to stare into his eyes, her heart turning over. His arm came up to circle her. He was going to…to…

Oh, God.

She exhaled sharply, feeling both relieved and annoyed as he reached around to try the knob.

He gave it a firm shake. "Have you got a screwdriver?"

"Get out."

"Lexy?" His bewildered look might have been cute some other time. "About the money. I'm just trying to make things legal. If I pay you back we can call it a loan, and no one can accuse us of anything later."

She wanted to laugh. And here she'd thought he was trying to help her. He was worried about his career.

Silly her. Sighing, she leaned against the wall and folded her arms across her chest. "You don't have to return the money. If anyone asks, I'll say whatever you want."

He was still too close, but it didn't matter anymore. Not now that she'd remembered she wasn't that besotted young fool who thought she could reform him.

"Tell me where to go tomorrow and I will be there," she said.

"I insist you take the money, Lexy." He wiggled the doorknob, ignoring her as if he had final say. "What about that screwdriver?"

Okay, now he was really irritating her. "I will give you one more chance to tell me where to go tomorrow before I tell you where—" memory of her friend's phrase momentarily failed her "—where to stick it."

His eyebrows rose. "What's wrong?"

"When I was nineteen and you were twenty-four, I thought your overbearing personality was cute." She pushed his hand away from the knob and managed to jerk open the door. "Now, I don't."

He narrowed his gaze. "I'm not overbearing. I'm being logical."

"Fine, Matthew. Kindly do it in your own home."

"Come on, Lex." He put his hand on her arm and his fingers lightly brushed her left breast.

She uncrossed her arms and shifted away. But it was too late. His innocent touch had sent an electric impulse straight to her core and nearly rattled the common sense right out of her.

Glaring at the offending hand, her gaze snagged on the gold Rolex watch circling his wrist. Tasha would be home in half an hour.

Lexy took a quick breath. No sense in cutting it too

close. She lifted her lashes, about to agree to any time, any place when his eyes met and held hers.

He'd felt the jolt, too. The telltale tic at his jaw told her even more than his heated gaze.

"Lexy?"

"Okay, tomorrow." She pushed forward, trying to force him out the door.

"I haven't given you the address yet," he said, not moving.

She raised her hands, tempted to bodily push him out. But his chest looked too solid, too inviting, and she balled her hands into fists and dropped them to her sides. "What is it?"

"It's 1020 Berkshire."

"I'll see you there."

He grunted when she crowded him over the door-jamb. "What time?"

He was doing it again, looking at her with those eyes, mesmerizing her, making her knees weak, her head fuzzy.

"Mommy." Tasha's high-pitched giggle pierced the fog. "What are you doing to that man?"

Lexy jumped back.

And met her daughter's wide, sapphire-blue eyes.

Chapter Two

Matthew stared at the dark-haired child, sickening shock mushrooming in his gut. She had to be about six or seven. Looking into her eyes was like looking into his own. The resemblance was purely coincidental. *It had to be.*

"Natasha." Lexy's hand flew to her chest. Her face was as white as death. "What are you doing home so early?"

A slightly hunched elderly woman stepped up behind the child and laid a protective hand on the girl's shoulder, her faded hazel eyes briefly sizing Matt up before turning to Lexy. "Her ballet teacher got ill. We thought we'd get Tasha a reading book and go back to my apartment so you can study."

"Oh, Mrs. Hershey, you've done enough already." Lexy's hand shook as she touched the woman's arm. "Really. I appreciate you taking her for me." She turned to her daughter. "Tasha, go inside." The child's mouth opened, and Lexy added, "Now."

"It's no trouble to keep her awhile longer," the other woman said. "Seeing as you have company." She gave Matthew a measuring glance.

"He was just leaving," Lexy said as she tugged at Tasha's sleeve.

Matthew found all three pairs of eyes on him. "I was...on my way out...this very minute." He moved farther into the hall, looking pointedly at Lexy. "Tomorrow?"

She nodded, pushing her daughter behind her. Tasha angled to the side and, poking her head out, smiled shyly at him, her clear blue eyes once again sending an arrow of panic to his chest.

He was being foolish. She couldn't possibly be his daughter. Lexy would have told him. She wasn't the type of woman to conceal something that important.

Half laughing at himself, he lifted a hand in farewell, but Lexy was already herding her daughter into their apartment. In the next second, the door slammed.

Across the hall, the elderly neighbor stood outside another apartment, her hand hovering on the knob, her face unsmiling. She gave him a long, unfriendly look before disappearing behind the door.

Nobody had to tell him he was persona non grata around here. Fine. All he wanted were those papers signed, and Lexy never had to see him again.

He continued down the hall toward the stairs, knowing from the trip up that the elevator was broken, and tried not to notice the peeling paint, the signs of wood rot along the baseboards. It wasn't the worst area of town, but the place was obviously falling apart. And he didn't like it that Lexy's doorknob was so flimsy. He'd noticed that she did have a fairly sturdy dead bolt, but for God's sake, she ought to at least have a doorknob that worked.

By the time he arrived at his late-model BMW, the guilt that was weighing his footsteps could be shoveled with a forklift. She was obviously supporting a daughter alone, she was still in school, her apartment was falling down around her ears, and he strongly suspected she didn't have a phone because she couldn't afford one.

Damn it. He was returning that money she'd given him seven years ago whether she liked it or not. He didn't care if she did see through his pretense. Repaying her wouldn't absolve him in the eyes of the law, but it would go a long way in easing his conscience.

He could do it, get her to take the money. He'd seen the fierce look on her face when it came to protecting her daughter. He smiled. She'd accept the repayment for Tasha's sake.

Thinking of the child again made him tingle with uneasiness. Lexy's eyes were brown. Tasha's were startlingly blue. Like his.

Settling into the leather passenger seat, he immediately lowered the air-conditioner temperature, then readjusted the vents to hit him face-on. He was uncomfortably warm. And not a little panicked as he thought back on that last night—their only night together.

They hadn't used protection. Their passion had been spontaneous, unexpected. He'd purposely tried to keep himself away from her for months during their short marriage, but in the end he'd blown it big-time. One brief taste of her softness, when she'd thrown her arms around him and told him she had received an A in English, and he'd lost it. Totally. Unforgivably.

He'd kicked himself for weeks afterward. He'd known Lexy wanted a life he wasn't prepared to give. But it had been too late. The damage had been done.

And not only had he ripped away her dreams, but he'd taken her virginity, too.

A scorpion's sting surely paled compared to the pain squeezing his chest as he remembered the look on her face when he said he was leaving.

He jammed the key into the ignition. He doubted Natasha was his daughter. But like any good lawyer, he had no intention of asking a question for which he didn't already know the answer.

Or then again, maybe he was just a coward.

The thought angered him, and he recklessly peeled the BMW away from the curb.

Either way, he'd make things right for Lexy. No matter what it took.

"YOU LOOK NICE," Mrs. Hershey said with an interested gleam in her eye when she came to take Tasha back to her apartment. "You doing something special after work?"

Lexy looked away. "No, I'll be home the same time as usual."

"I don't mind keeping Tasha longer if you'd like to go out." The older woman smiled. "A young person like you needs to have fun sometimes."

Lexy returned the smile. "Thanks, but honestly, the only reason I wore this—" she plucked at the yellow cotton sundress, a splurge she'd worn only once before on a rare date two years ago—a disastrous date, one she couldn't forget fast enough "—is because I need to do laundry."

Color heated her cheeks at the small fib, and she turned to get Tasha's dinner out of the refrigerator. She wasn't trying to impress Matthew. He'd already seen how pathetic she could look, had witnessed the sad state of her apartment. But she just didn't want him to think…well, she wasn't sure what she wanted him to think.

She placed an apple and a covered dish on the counter. "I have a snack for Tasha and dinner here for both of you. She doesn't get any dessert because she had too much sugar today."

Mrs. Hershey made a clucking sound with her tongue. "You are so stubborn, Lexy. I don't know why you don't let me feed her. She eats like a bird."

She smiled at the compassionate woman who was on a fixed income herself but was always trying to shower them with extra food under the pretense of having cooked too much. Lexy hated to lie to her, even a little. But she didn't want to have to explain about Matthew. Besides, after she signed the papers this afternoon, she'd never see him again.

Lexy took a deep breath and reminded herself that not seeing him again was a very good thing. And him never seeing Natasha again was even better.

The fact that he'd shown not a hint of recognition when he saw her daughter should have relieved Lexy. And it did. But it made her furious, too. He was just as callous and self-centered as she remembered. She'd been right not to tell him about Tasha. For all his faults, she knew he would have tried to do the right thing by them had he known. And he would have hated her the rest of his life for it.

Tamping down a sigh, she started to bag the food, knowing she'd worried for nothing. She really should have known better. Matthew had made it all too clear that he didn't want a family. Even if he'd had the slightest suspicion that Tasha was his, he'd probably gone straight into denial.

"Remember, dear, if you decide that you want to stay out a little later tonight, just give me a ring and I'll tuck Tasha in on my sofa."

Lexy smiled her gratitude, even though she knew she wouldn't be accepting the offer, then called for her daughter to get out of the bathroom. Tasha was in week three of her hair-decorating phase and often took an hour to get ready.

When all she got was a mumbled "Coming," she glanced at Mrs. Hershey. "Two more minutes and I will drag her out."

The other woman laughed. "I'm in no hurry. Oprah doesn't start for another half hour."

The doorbell rang and Lexy's pulse skidded. She had absolutely no reason to think it was Matthew again. But she supposed she'd have this reaction for the next couple of weeks, just as she had when the pizza-delivery man had rung her bell in error last night, and the kid selling magazine subscriptions had this morning.

When she opened the door, a young man stopped jerking to the music presumably coming from his headphones. Squinting at a brown envelope, he said, "I have a telegram for Alessandra Monroe."

Lexy winced. Addressed to Alessandra, it could only be from one person. She accepted the envelope and gave him a smile when he probably expected a tip. But he just grinned back, adjusted his headphones, then started boogying toward the stairs.

"I hope it's not bad news," Mrs. Hershey said, her hand fluttering to her throat as soon as Lexy returned to the kitchen.

"Oh, no. It's probably from my parents in Hungary. They contact me this way sometimes." Except they normally wrote letters. With a nagging feeling that she wasn't going to like what she found, she tore open the envelope.

Quickly she scanned the Hungarian words.

And belatedly realized she should have sat down first.

"What's the matter, child?" Mrs. Hershey hurried around the counter to cup Lexy's elbow. "You look a little green."

"I'm okay." She swallowed. "It is from my parents. They're coming to visit."

Her friend's eyebrows furrowed. "I thought you got on well with them."

"I do. This is just such a surprise." She swept a morose glance around the shabby apartment. They were never going to understand.

"You told me they might come eventually."

"But I didn't think they really would." Lexy stared down at her hands. "I haven't been totally truthful with them."

"Ah." Mrs. Hershey patted her arm. "Do they know about Natasha?"

Slowly Lexy nodded and gave her neighbor a sheepish look. "But they think I'm married."

"Oh."

"And that I live in a big house."

Mrs. Hershey's eyebrows rose slightly.

"And that I've finished school."

Her friend frowned.

Lexy sniffed. "And that I have a terrific job."

"I see," the other woman said, amusement curving the corners of her mouth. "You've been just a *little* untruthful, huh?"

Lexy closed her eyes and half laughed, half sobbed. "I'm in trouble."

Mrs. Hershey put an arm around her. "When are they coming?"

"In one week."

"Oh, my."

"Yes." Lexy's voice caught. "It's really complicated." She paused, not sure how much she wanted to reveal. "They used most of their savings to send me here and I didn't want—I can't disappoint them. I—they—"

The other woman patted her arm. "You don't owe me an explanation."

Natasha took care of any further discussion by rounding the corner and beaming at Lexy. Today her dark brown hair was bound by three ribbons, one yellow, one pink and the third a bright turquoise. A short laugh escaped Lexy. Tasha's grandparents were going to love her. She definitely pulled the Gypsy blood.

Again the doorbell rang.

"I'll get it," Tasha called.

"You're not allowed to—" Lexy started to remind her just as her daughter flung open the door.

"Matthew?" Lexy's eyes widened on him, then her gaze darted to her daughter, then back to him. She motioned for Tasha to come to her. "What are you doing here?"

"Hi." He shrugged shoulders that looked no less broad with the absence of his suit coat. Today he wore a burgundy polo shirt that did amazing things to his blue eyes and sun-streaked hair. In one hand he held a legal-size envelope. The other hand gripped the yellow handle of a screwdriver.

"Mrs. Hershey—?" Lexy turned beseeching eyes to her friend.

The woman stopped her with a raised blue-veined hand. "Tasha and I have a date with Oprah. Come on, honey," she said, and lowered her hand to take Tasha's.

Normally shy around strangers, her daughter started to jut her lips out in a stubborn pout, her free hand going to her hip.

Lexy gave her the eye. The one that said this was not open to discussion.

Tasha wrinkled her nose. "You have to meet all of *my* friends."

"He's not my friend," Lexy said automatically, her gaze flicking to Matthew before fixing sternly on her daughter. "This is business. Now go."

"Yeah, but—"

Lexy let out a string of Hungarian that made her daughter straighten. She didn't understand the words but knew her mother meant business. Abruptly she turned toward Mrs. Hershey's apartment. The older woman chuckled as she unlocked her door and let them in.

Lexy waited until she heard the lock click before she turned to glare at Matthew. "What are you doing here?"

"Could you teach me that?" His lips were curved in that smile that normally made her knees weak.

Not today. She folded her arms across her chest. "I was supposed to meet you at your office."

He held up the envelope. "I brought the paperwork."

"I don't want you coming around here."

Nodding, he slid a glance at Mrs. Hershey's closed

door before meeting her eyes. "Since I'm already here, can I come in?"

There was that cocky sureness in his face, and she was tempted to tell him no. It would take only seconds to scrawl her signature. She could do it right here.

Clearly he sensed her hesitation. The cockiness began to slip and he said, "You may have some questions. Shall we go somewhere to discuss them?"

Irritation simmered in her chest. He was right. She'd be a fool to sign anything she hadn't read. She'd been on her own and responsible for herself and Tasha for too long to be that careless. Besides, what reason did she have to trust him?

Without a word, she stepped to the side, her gaze briefly lingering on the screwdriver he still had in his hand.

"You look nice," he said as he moved past her, his spicy male scent making her wish she hadn't stayed so close. Halfway into the room he stopped and faced her, his expression slightly alarmed. "Not that you didn't look nice yesterday."

She laughed. "I know what I looked like yesterday, Matthew." Oh, no. She hoped he didn't think she'd dressed up for him. Or had blow-dried her hair just so. Or had taken a half hour to apply her makeup…

"I work today," she added quickly, glancing at her bare wrist and mentioning the diner where she waitressed. "In fact, I have to be there soon, so we'd better get this taken care of."

She refused to look at him, and when her gaze drew to the kitchen counter, she noticed that yesterday's bills were still strewn around. She motioned him toward the sofa and rushed to sweep the papers into one stack, turned over, in the corner.

When she turned around, Matthew wasn't in the living room. He'd returned to the door and was inspecting the knob. He inserted the screwdriver and gave it a couple of quick turns.

Without looking up, he shook the knob. It wobbled only slightly. "This is better, but you really ought to get this replaced," he said, finally looking in her direction. "Don't you have a building superintendent?"

"Sure, but he's having lunch with the doorman."

He gave her a wry look.

She sighed. "The rent is cheap. If we have a small problem, we take care of it ourselves."

"This isn't a small problem. This is about security."

"Thank you for your concern." She held out her hand. "The papers?"

Frowning, he obliged her, then followed her into the living room. She sat on the recliner and he took the couch.

"Your daughter's a cute kid," he said, and the papers in Lexy's hand rattled.

"Yes." Her gaze darted up to meet his. "Thank you," she murmured, taking a deep breath and switching her attention to the small stack of papers stapled together. She had to get rid of him. "I really don't have to read these. I trust you."

He hesitated. "Okay."

"Let me find a pen."

"Here you go." He held out a gold-colored one.

She scooted forward to accept it, and when her eyes flicked to his face, she saw him staring at her breasts. He quickly looked away, his jaw clenched.

Casting a furtive glance downward, she saw that her sundress was gaping, evidencing her braless condition.

She sank back. The recliner's loose spring jabbed her hip. She wasn't upset that he'd looked. It was a natural reaction. The sudden heat searing her belly was what disturbed her. The way her body instantly remembered his hot mouth on her skin.

Her nervous hands fumbled with the papers until she saw the line for her signature. She positioned the pen and had touched it to the paper when the word *alimony* caught her eye.

Her hand froze. She blinked.

Alimony.

The word was vaguely familiar, but she couldn't quite translate it.

"Is something wrong?" Matthew asked.

She stared at the document. "Maybe I should read this."

Silence stretched. "Probably." He exhaled loudly. "I don't want to get into an argument about this, Lexy."

She looked him squarely in the eyes. "Why would we?"

"Because you're stubborn and you're not going to want to take the money."

She had a pretty good idea of what *alimony* meant now. She tried to hand his pen back to him. "You're right."

He wouldn't take it. "Look, if you won't do it for yourself, accept it for Tasha's sake."

"My daughter is none of your business."

"I know that."

Did he? A shiver raised goose bumps on her skin. "We're doing just fine. Her father is faithful about sending her child support." The lie tumbled from her lips before she had a chance to consider the consequences, and her insides trembled with the realization.

Surprise, then relief registered across his face.

She seriously wanted to smack him.

"I'm glad to hear that," he said, and she had to bite back the sarcastic remark ready to leap from her tongue. "I know that's a problem for many single mothers."

She gave him a curt nod, her anger slipping into sadness. "So, you see, we don't have that problem."

His smile was slow, a little glum, and in a subdued voice he said, "Take the money, Lexy."

Their gazes locked.

She swallowed. She could take his arrogance, his desire to succeed...she could even take his rejection. But she couldn't take his kindness. And certainly not his pity.

"It's really your money. It's not as though I'm handing it to you," he said softly. "Can't we consider it a loan repaid?"

She looked away then, her gaze homing in on the warped kitchen floor. Her walls were peeling, the refrigerator was ready to die and they ate on their laps because she couldn't afford a table and chairs. Not that they had spare room for any more furniture.

She bit her lip. No wonder he pitied her. Still, they were okay. One more semester and she'd be done with school. Then things would be different for her and Tasha.

Taking a deep breath, she summoned a smile and started to turn to him. Her attention caught on the brown telegram lying on the counter.

Her parents.

They were going to see all this.

And know she'd lied to them for seven years.

Her pulse started to race as she switched her attention to Matthew, the short, rehearsed line of polite refusal already dying in her head.

A crazier thought replaced it, as a kernel of insanity began to grow and take root.

"I do need a favor," she said, letting the pros and cons mentally face off. He'd already denied Tasha. That was the most important problem solved. Her heart pounded. This could work.

His face lit with satisfaction and he leaned toward her. "Anything."

She put down the pen and refolded the papers. Wariness darkened his expression as he watched her stuff the documents back into the envelope.

"Relax, Matthew," she said, brightly. "I only need a husband for two more weeks."

Chapter Three

"I'm not following you," Matt said, dread slithering down his spine. He looked at her unsteady hands. She'd closed the envelope without signing the divorce papers.

"I need you to pretend you're still my husband." She lifted her chin, her expression blank. "And that you're Tasha's father. But you won't have to spend any time with her," she added quickly.

He shook his head. "You are making absolutely no sense."

"I know." She worried her lower lip with her teeth. "Give me a minute to gather my thoughts."

This wasn't good. Her accent was stronger. She made little agitated movements with her hands. Above the top of her dress, her skin was flushed, the color slowly making its way to her face. She seemed excited, maybe a little afraid.

Her serious brown eyes met his.

And determined. She was definitely determined.

What the hell had he gotten himself into?

He cleared his throat. "Uh, Lexy, you forgot to sign the papers."

She set them aside and leaned forward, clasping her

hands together and resting them just above her knees. "Two weeks, Matthew, that's all I need. I promise."

She still had terrific legs. Smooth, golden, slim ankles. They were strong, too, he remembered.

He cursed to himself. Those kinds of memories he didn't need. He lifted his gaze...and came in direct view of her breasts. They were pretty terrific, too.

He closed his eyes and pinched the bridge of his nose. "Lexy, you still haven't told me what this is about."

"My parents are coming, and they think we're still married."

He lowered his hand. "From Hungary?"

She nodded, looking miserable. "They don't know much about you, so it shouldn't be hard." Lifting her shoulder in a small shrug, she said, "Actually, they think I'm married to this wonderful man."

He snorted. "Thanks."

She shrugged again and looked a little sheepish, but made no attempt to retract her statement.

"It can't work." He tried to ignore the bruising his ego had just taken. She'd thought he was pretty wonderful once. Of course that was before he'd run like a hyena.

"Yes, it can."

"No way," he said, shaking his head and watching uncertainty pucker her forehead. He paused for a moment, his suspicion growing as sharp as a new pencil. "You haven't thought this through, have you?"

"It will be easy, Matthew. You will only have to see them twice, maybe three times."

"Really?"

"Yes. We will say you are away on business for

one week. They already think you are a very important man.''

He straightened. Damn it. He *was* important. But that was a moot point. This wasn't going to work. He could poke a dozen holes in her plan. "What about Tasha? She can't start calling some strange man Daddy.''

Lexy gave a startled jerk. "Of course not. But my parents don't speak English. Only my brother does, and he isn't coming.'' She spread her hands in a helpless gesture. "You will only meet them twice. For dinner. They eat very late. Tasha will already be asleep.''

He hated to be patronizing, but it was obvious she hadn't mapped this plan out. He smiled indulgently. "I know this is hard for you and I'm sure—''

"Everything will work out fine,'' she said finishing for him, and folded her arms across her chest with finality. Her dress bunched and gaped and he got an excellent shot of two creamy swells.

Instantly he recalled the way her breasts had fit in his hands, the way they'd tasted. His body tensed as if it were yesterday that she'd slipped into his bed. She'd offered him more temptation than he'd been able to resist.

Yeah, right. *This* would work.

He passed a weary hand over his face. "Lexy, be reasonable.''

"Did you or did you not say 'anything'?''

He squinted, thinking back for a moment. She was referring to his offer. Hell, didn't she realize that was a figure of speech?

"What I meant—''

She cut him off with a huff of exasperation. "You

meant money. You wanted to—to—'' Her accent intensified as she struggled for the right words. Uncrossing her arms and waving an impatient hand through the air, she ended with "Buy me off."

"That is not true and I resent your accusation."

She opened her mouth, closed it again, then said, "Tough."

He didn't know what to say to that. He laughed. *Tough?* Lexy certainly had changed. So had her vocabulary.

"This is not a joke, Matthew. I want you to pretend we're still married for two weeks."

"We *are* still married," he reminded her dryly.

"Exactly." A triumphant smile tugged at the corners of her mouth. "So this should be no problem."

"I'm engaged. Remember?"

"We won't be doing anything…marital," she snapped.

"I know that." He left the couch to look out the window, a restless energy making him suddenly irritable. The street below was filthy with litter, and someone's feet were poking out of a cardboard box down the alley across from the apartment.

When he thought he heard a sniffle, he turned back to Lexy, but she sat there dry-eyed, watching him. "I won't make this hard, Matthew, I promise. I won't expect you to be around much. In fact, it would be better that you aren't."

He faced the window again, tempted to ask her why. Was it because he wasn't the wonderful husband she'd written her parents about? That was stupid. Stupid because he even half cared. And stupid because being around too much would eventually tip them off to the deception. That was her concern.

Against his better judgment, he slid her another glance. She looked so damned pretty in that yellow dress. Sweet, too, and innocent, just as he remembered her. He didn't want to have to tell her no. She'd been a good sport about him suddenly showing up after being such a jerk seven years ago. But then there was Amanda. If she found out about this...

Lexy took a deep breath as she waited patiently for him to say something, and his attention once again was drawn to the hypnotic rhythm of her breasts rising and falling. She seemed fuller, more filled out than he remembered. Having a child probably had done that.

This was going to be one of his bigger mistakes. He rammed a hand through his hair. "Where will they sleep?"

She straightened, and he forced himself to stop looking at her tightened neckline. "You will do it?"

"I'm considering it. But let's iron out the facts first."

She nodded, her distracted expression not reassuring him. "Let's see...sleeping arrangements...I hadn't really thought that out yet." She shrugged. "A motel. There's one not too far from here."

"Good," he said, and noticed the worried way she was biting her lip. He pretty much knew she didn't have any money. And from what he recalled, he doubted her parents had much, either. "I'll pay for it."

Her eyes widened on him. "You will not."

He held up a warning hand. "You've forgotten who's holding the trump card."

Confusion creased her face.

A smile lifted one side of his mouth. They used to go through this translation process a lot. "If you want me to play, you have to let me make some of the rules.''

''Oh, you mean you're threatening me.''

''I wouldn't call it that.''

She thought in silence for a moment. ''So, if I said I wouldn't sign the divorce papers unless you do this for me, that would not be considered a threat, either?''

Sitting with her hands clasped, her expression was so innocent, so serene, that it stopped him. Did she know what she was saying?

She shrugged, a ghost of a smile playing around her lips. ''I guess I have one of your trump cards, yes?''

Matt scrubbed at his eyes. When had this problem gotten so complicated? When had his sweet, shy Lexy turned into such a little fiend? He should have let Brad do his dirty work. Then Brad could play the adoring husband.

Not a soothing thought.

''My fiancée can't know about this,'' Matt said, in total disbelief over what he was about to agree to. ''You said two dinners. That's it. Right?''

''Right.''

''What about Tasha's father? Will he be a problem?

A fearful gleam entered Lexy's eyes. ''How?''

This wasn't good. The guy could be some loose cannon for all Matt knew. ''Is he going to show up and slug me for claiming to be Tasha's father?''

She blinked, looking startled…uneasy…amused. ''No.''

''Lexy,'' he said, drawing out her name in warning. ''It's fair for me to know what I'm getting into. If Tasha says anything to him—''

Looking down at her hands, she said, ''Tasha has never met her father.''

"You're kidding."

"So you have nothing to worry about."

"But you said he pays child support."

She kept her gaze glued to her hands. "Why is this important?"

His earlier relief began to falter. "Tell me about him."

Bitter sadness briefly filled her eyes as she looked up. "He is a selfish, ambitious, uncaring man. And Tasha is better off without him. So don't feel sorry for either of us."

He let out a long, slow breath and reclaimed his place on the couch without looking at her. His thoughts scattered like a handful of ticker tape. No need to analyze this now. He'd be better off accepting Lexy's explanation. Skepticism would serve no purpose.

He swung his attention back to her and didn't miss the resentful glance she gave him before turning to look out the window. Or had that been his imagination?

Maybe he should ask Brad to do him this favor.

Lexy was different now. She was stronger, older, more worldly. She could handle Brad.

"You're changing your mind," she said quietly, her gaze still focused on something outside. "It's okay."

She bowed her head to study the envelope containing their divorce papers. Several seconds later, she picked up the pen and started to withdraw the documents.

Matt immediately stood and pried them from her icy-cold fingers. He'd walked out on her once before. He wouldn't do it again.

LEXY HATED BEING LATE for anything. Especially work. But Tasha was being unusually difficult this afternoon, first fussing with her hair, then searching for her pink shorts and matching striped T-shirt that Lexy had twice explained were still in the dryer.

The groceries had barely been put away and now her daughter was unloading the refrigerator in hot pursuit of "purple juice." Lexy massaged the tension throbbing at her temple. She'd forgotten to buy aspirin again.

"Three more minutes, young lady, or I'll miss my bus," she called to Tasha as she dashed into their shared bedroom for her purse.

"What about my shorts and shirt?"

"Mrs. Hershey will pull them out of the dryer in fifteen minutes." Lexy tried to keep the impatience out of her voice as she rushed back to the kitchen to grab her name tag off the counter.

It wasn't her daughter's fault that she'd been on edge since her meeting with Matthew yesterday. Although Tasha hadn't exactly been an angel, either. As much as Lexy was trying not to think about Matthew, the child had a million questions about him. Trivial questions. Stubborn questions. Endless ones. Until Lexy was ready to scream.

"Then how can I wear them now?"

"You can't." She crouched down to adjust Tasha's wrinkled collar. "Please, honey, I can't be late a second day in a row. This outfit looks very pretty on you."

"But, Mommy," she whined, drawing out the word. "It's too tight."

Lexy closed her eyes and sighed. Guilt made her throat go dry. Six-year-olds seemed to grow out of their clothes overnight. When she lifted her lashes, she smiled at Tasha. "Maybe we can go shopping for a few things next payday. Would you like that?"

Angling her head to the side, Tasha gave a reluctant nod, a tiny smile starting to form on her face. "Do you think we can go before that man comes over again?"

So Tasha had a childish crush on Matthew, just as Lexy had suspected. Terrific. "Sure, honey." She glanced at the clock and quickly restored the few items Tasha had left out of the fridge. "Ready?"

Lexy quickly left her with Mrs. Hershey who was waiting at her apartment door, then flew down the stairs and hoped to heaven she hadn't already missed her bus.

She made it on time, but only by seconds, and ended up having to stand due to the lack of seats. The air conditioner wasn't working for the third day in a row, and she edged past the crowd to get as close to an open window as possible.

It was going to be a long evening on her feet, and she hadn't slept but three hours last night before going to her janitorial job at the school this morning. Not a great way to prepare for her finals, but she had too much to think about. Like how she was going to get away with her crazy scheme.

If not for her parents' inability to speak English, she wouldn't have a prayer at all. Good thing Hungarian wasn't a popular language in Ohio. They'd have to largely depend on what she told them.

But she still had two major concerns—Tasha and the apartment. At some point, Tasha would have to interact with Matthew in front of her parents, no matter how briefly. Making sure their contact was confined to a bedtime tuck-in would make things simpler. And as much as Lexy felt ashamed for not having taught her daughter much Hungarian, she was grateful now that she hadn't. Without traumatizing her daughter, it would be easy to have Tasha call Matthew Popo, as Lexy had called her own father at that age. She could tell Tasha it was Matthew's nickname.

The apartment problem was more pressing. She lived in a dump. There was no getting around that fact. Her parents were going to be horrified. But short of moving into the motel with them, which was becoming a serious possibility for her, she wasn't sure what else she could do. Asking Matthew for any additional help was out of the question. Besides, God forbid that his fiancée should find out....

Busy feeling cranky, Lexy nearly missed her stop and almost landed in someone's lap in her panic to pull the cord. She yanked hard and the bus lurched to a stop. Giving her fellow passengers an apologetic smile, she scooted off the bus and ran the half block to the restaurant.

"Better step on it," Laurie whispered. "Sweet Cheeks is in one of his moods." The waitress swept by her, carrying a loaded tray high in one hand as Lexy hurried past the register.

Lexy kept an eye on her boss's back as he stood stocking the display shelves behind the lunch counter, then headed for the back room where she could stash her purse and get a fresh apron.

"One minute and counting," Mel said without turning around. "Hope this ain't turning into a habit."

As usual, his baggy black pants were sagging hopelessly off his nonexistent butt, which had earned him the name Sweet Cheeks. Lexy had no idea how this image prompted the name, but the thought always made her grin.

"Forty seconds, Mel, and I'll be at my station," she called over her shoulder. She rarely paid any attention to his gruff manner. Inside he was a pussycat. Not that she'd tell him that to his face, she thought with a wry smile.

The next four hours were a blur of customers and heaping plates of fried chicken and the pot roast special. Last count, Lexy guessed she'd also served close to twenty orders of apple cobbler. And she had the sore feet to prove it.

Massaging her lower back, she watched the crowd start to thin, then waited for Laurie to come back from her cigarette break before going to pour herself a cup of coffee.

She'd just taken her first sip when she heard the bells over the door jingle. Flexing a stiff shoulder from carrying heavy trays, she turned, fervently hoping it was a parting customer and not a new one.

Lexy blinked at the sight of Matthew's shoulders filling the doorway. His navy blue sport coat looked tailor-made, his khakis were perfectly creased. He'd worried about his appearance even in law school.

"Hubba hubba," Laurie whispered behind her. "Come to Mama."

Lexy sent a weak grin over her shoulder. "He's not your type."

"Honey, for half an hour, they're all my type."

Lexy laughed, no longer shocked by the younger woman's brassy remarks. After working with her for three years, Lexy had grown used to them. She'd even picked up some of the phrases. In fact, Laurie had taught her a lot of American slang. "Trust me on this one. He *really* isn't your type."

Laurie arched an over-plucked red eyebrow. "You know him?"

"I'm afraid so." Lexy sighed, put down her coffee and started toward Matthew.

As soon as he spotted her, a truly magnificent smile lit his face, and her foolish heart fluttered. "I was hoping I'd catch you," he said.

"What do you want, Matthew?"

His smile dissolved into a quick frown. "I figured I'd give you a ride home. Then we could discuss our—" He cut himself short, his gaze straying over her shoulder.

Lexy didn't have to turn around to know Laurie was eavesdropping. It would be just like her. "Why don't you take a booth," she said. "I'll be off in half an hour. I'll get you some coffee in the meantime."

"Uh, do you have cappuccino?"

Her gaze briefly swept the dusty silk plants, the red vinyl booths, the Formica-top lunch counter, before she gave him a bland look. "What do you think?"

Rubbing his clean-shaven jaw, he threw an uncomfortable glance around the room. "Coffee will be fine."

She moved away as he slid into a booth, and tried not to think about how hopeless her plan was. She and Matthew were like fire and rain, apple cobbler and crêpe suzettes…cappuccino and decaf. And her parents. Oh, heavens. She didn't think she could possibly prepare him for them.

She automatically brought him cream with his coffee, amazed that she still remembered after all these years. When their eyes briefly met, she knew he'd noticed, too.

Frowning, he asked, "Do you always take a bus home this late?"

She nodded. "Yup. Tasha and I have developed a nasty habit. We like to eat."

He turned to stare at the darkness outside the plate-glass windows, and she privately admitted that she would be awfully glad for the ride home. Her feet hurt and her headache still hadn't completely gone away since this afternoon. And in all honesty, having Matthew concerned enough to want to take her home was kind of nice.

"Surely you can find a job closer to home," he said, his gaze turning back to the simple but properly set tables, the few remaining blue-collar-type customers. "It's not like this place is the—"

His attention had returned to her face, her murderous gaze stopping him cold. "Don't feel as though you have to wait around."

She started to turn away, but he grabbed her forearm. "Come on, Lexy, you're jumping to conclusions. I only meant that tips here can't be so good that you couldn't find some place closer to home."

She shook away. "I know exactly what you meant, Matthew," she said in a lowered voice, still seething but trying to remain calm. A couple in the adjacent booth had turned to stare.

"This isn't like you, Lexy."

That did it. She was going to march back to the counter, grab the pot of coffee and dump the entire thing on his lap. "How would you know?" she asked first, and was pleased to see dread eclipse his expression. "You didn't stick around long enough to get to know me, did you?

"Not that I care," she added quickly. "Three months of your opinionated, arrogant, snobby, I'm-so-wonderful attitude was more than enough. But don't come charging into my life now, thinking you know me. You don't."

He stared in disbelief, his surprise evident in the stunned glaze of his eyes, the wordless parting of his mouth.

"The list is longer," she added peevishly, then felt the shame seep into her complexion. She'd already said enough. Especially for someone who claimed not to care.

"Go on, if it'll make you feel better," he said, and her shame slid to anger.

"I won't waste my breath," she said with a small lift of her chin.

"God forbid."

She frowned, not quite sure what that meant.

"I think you're equating confidence with arrogance," he said in a calm, reasonable voice that annoyed rather than soothed her. "And as far as being snobby, I have always believed that if you stick with winners, which is to say high achievers, you'll be a winner. The theory has to do with pushing oneself to greater heights. I'm sorry you choose to misunderstand that concept."

Lexy wished she had already gone for the coffeepot. High achievers. Ha. She could only imagine what he thought of this place and its clientele. She was surprised he'd even dirtied the bottom of his shoes by walking in here.

She cast a quick glance around the room. She knew

more than half of the remaining customers. They were all good, hard-working people who often came in to eat with their families. Definitely not part of his social circle, but she considered them winners.

A blonde in the far corner stood suddenly. Lexy didn't recognize her, and she cringed slightly when a nasty thought crossed her mind. The woman was between bleach jobs, dressed like she conducted business two street corners down and was probably typical of the kind of person Matthew expected to find here. Luckily, his back was half to the woman and he probably hadn't seen her.

Lexy shook away the unkind thought and turned to Matthew. "I'm not going to argue with you."

He held up both hands in surrender. "I have no intention of arguing. I do enough of that in court."

"Matthew? Matthew Monroe?" The blonde stopped at the table, leaned over, her heaving breasts nearly popping out of her tight, shiny gold blouse. "I thought that was you," she said, and threw her arms around him.

His mouth dropped open in surprise...a second before she landed a big red smooch.

Chapter Four

Matthew slid across the seat and out of Mrs. Hornsby's clutches. However, her cigarette-scented breath lingered, and he struggled not to cringe in disgust.

"Matthew." Her lower lip jutted in a petulant pout and she planted a hand on one slim hip. "It's Taffy. I know you remember."

"Of course." He didn't bother to look at Lexy, who still hovered nearby. He could easily picture her wide brown eyes, lit with both shock and amusement. "How are you, Mrs. Hornsby?"

She eyed the spot he'd vacated in his haste to escape, and he quickly slid over again and started to get out of the booth. No way would he let her corner him in. The guys in the office didn't call her Horny Hornsby for nothing.

"Mrs. Hornsby?" she repeated with a mocking look that made him want to crawl under the table. "After all we've been through together, you call me Mrs. Hornsby."

He forced a smile. "Taffy, meet Lexy." He glanced at Lexy then, and she looked so much like his old Lexy—wide-eyed, innocent, beautiful—that he momentarily lost his train of thought. His gaze slid back to Taffy and he said quickly, "Mrs. Hornsby used to be a client of mine."

Taffy sent a brief smile Lexy's way before giving him her full attention. "Hmm, that's right. I'm not really a client anymore now that old lard-butt finally paid up."

The name she called her ex-husband made one side of Matt's mouth curve. She was no doubt one of his most colorful clients. One who'd earned him a hefty fee after he'd gotten the former stripper an impressive settlement from her elderly millionaire husband.

After a moment's pause, she said, "I guess this puts us on the same playing field, doesn't it? I mean, you can't use the 'not mixing business with pleasure' excuse anymore." She advanced a step.

Like a true coward, his gaze skittered to Lexy for help.

"May I get you two some coffee? A bottle of wine?" she asked, a small grin tugging at her mouth.

Matt had a good notion to leave and let her catch the damn bus. "Uh, no, thanks. You are about ready, aren't you, Lexy?"

Taffy blinked, then turned toward Lexy with new interest. She eyed the smaller woman dressed in the simple pink uniform, and her shoulders went back two subtle degrees, causing her phenomenal breasts to thrust forward.

Matt clenched and unclenched his jaw. "Lexy?"

From behind them, someone cleared his throat. Matt turned as a beefy man with a gruff voice said, "Go ahead, Lexy, punch out. I'll take it from here."

Lexy folded her arms across her chest and did nothing to hide her surprised amusement. "Oh, Mel, I wouldn't think of deserting you this way."

"Beat it, kid," he said under his breath, except Matt heard, and he gave Lexy the eye to listen to the guy.

She gave them each an incredibly annoying smile and waited for several long seconds before she said, "Okay."

Mel immediately turned to Taffy, pulled out the cigar hanging from the corner of his mouth and grinned. "What can I get you?"

Matt watched the hypnotic sway of Lexy's hips as she strolled leisurely toward the back of the restaurant. She'd filled out nicely in the past seven years, although she was still a little too thin. Then he remembered the pleasant way her breasts had held up that sundress and...

He gave an involuntary grunt at the jab he took in his ribs and turned to Taffy, who was poised for another attack.

"Are you listening to me?" she asked, letting her arm relax.

"Sorry," he mumbled, and glanced at Mel, who'd stuck his cigar back into his mouth. While Matt had been distracted, Taffy had shot the guy down. He knew that look of rejection.

"Do you have a date with this girl, or what?" she asked.

Matt frowned at Mel, who looked far too interested in his answer. "Bet you have some coffee to pour."

Mel grunted and shuffled off in the same direction as Lexy had gone.

"No," Matt said. "She's an old friend. I'm giving her a ride."

Taffy wrinkled her nose. "I'm not stupid, Matthew."

He didn't want to know what that meant. "How's your new business going?"

At the diversionary tactic, a wry smile curved her mouth. "Slow, but I'm sticking with it."

"Good. Good. Well, nice seeing you again," he said, and extended a hand.

Her smile broadening, she accepted the handshake. "If it doesn't work out between you two, you know my number."

"It's not what you think—"

She laughed. "Yeah, sure. All I can say is, you never looked at me that way."

He thought briefly about denying the charge, then figured it was best to let it go when she gave him a smug wink. He frowned when he realized she wasn't winking at *him*.

Turning, he found Lexy standing there.

Oh, hell. How much had she heard? "Are you ready?"

Slipping off her name tag with one hand, she held up her purse with the other.

"Let's go." With a nod to Taffy, he hurried Lexy out of the diner and steered her toward his car. He unlocked the passenger door, opened it, and when their eyes met, he held up his free hand. "Don't say it."

"I have no idea what you're talking about," she said as she slid into the seat.

"She was a client for my firm," he said, climbing in behind the wheel.

"So you've said."

"That was it."

"I didn't think anything different."

He started the engine and slid a look at her shadowed profile. "Well, it's kind of funny that we were just talking about hanging out with winners."

She turned to him, and a streetlight illuminated the puzzled look on her face.

He chuckled. "And then Taffy pops up."

Something that seemed like disappointment turned down the corners of her mouth. "It's not my place to judge her."

"You know what I meant."

Her brief smile was sad. "Did I thank you for the ride?"

"No problem." He pulled out into traffic, suddenly wishing he'd waited for her at her apartment. She was making him feel like a heel, and he didn't need the aggravation. He was having enough trouble coming up with excuses to put off his fiancée for two weeks. It wasn't as if he was putting down Taffy Hornsby. He'd only...she just wasn't...

Damn.

"Open the glove compartment," he ordered gruffly. "I have something in there for you."

Ignoring his high-handedness, she did as he asked. "This?"

He pulled his gaze from the road for a moment. She held the slim, state-of-the-art cellular phone as though she didn't know what to do with it. "You just flip it open. Press Power, the number you want to call, then Send. It's simple."

"Why would I need this?"

"Because you don't have a phone."

She shook her head and tucked the unit back into the glove box. "I've already told you I won't accept your charity."

"Charity, hell. I can't come chasing you down every time I need to talk to you. This is for my convenience, not yours."

She paused. "Oh."

He leaned back in the deep leather seat and exhaled. It was half-true. "There's a recharger in there, too. You can keep it plugged in at home, but keep the phone in your purse."

"Okay, but…"

"Look," he said, guessing at her hesitancy. "Don't worry about the bill. I'm taking care of it. Like I said, this arrangement is for my convenience."

"Of course."

At her chilly tone, he stretched out the tension building in the side of his neck. "Feel free to use it for your personal calls, as well."

Her silence was not reassuring.

"Look," he said, "are we going to be able to talk at your place or do you want to stop for a drink?"

"I have to pick up Tasha at Mrs. Hershey's."

"Try out your new phone. I bet your neighbor won't mind keeping her an extra hour."

She sighed. "I don't like to take advantage of her. She's good enough to watch Tasha, and I have to argue with her to accept what little money I can afford to give her as it is."

He started to offer to pay Mrs. Hershey an additional sum for her trouble, but wisely decided to keep his mouth shut. Lexy wouldn't appreciate it. And he didn't blame her. She was proud and stubborn, and he had a lot of respect for the way she was struggling to bring up her daughter on her own. If anyone would end up raising a well-adjusted child despite the challenging odds, Lexy would.

Matt slid her an appreciative glance. It had been a while since he'd run across anyone who didn't use money to fix their problems. So much for his circle of friends.

"I could wait until you get Tasha to sleep, and then come up," he said instead.

She laid her head back against the seat. "You don't have to wait. She needs to get used to you. Of course, it may take longer to get her to fall asleep if she knows you're there," she said, and he thought he heard a smile in her voice. "She has a crush on you."

"Natasha?" He nearly ran a stop sign but slowed the car just in time. "No kidding? Is that normal for a girl that age?"

Lexy laughed. "These days they're ready to get married at twelve."

"That isn't funny. I hope you don't—" He stopped, embarrassed that he felt compelled to preach. And shocked that he felt the urge at all. What the hell did he know about kids? Exactly what he wanted to know. Nothing.

"Encourage marriage?" Lexy asked. "Careful, Matthew, you're going to put yourself out of business."

"I doubt that. Anyway, that wasn't what I was going to say. Obviously I have nothing against the institution."

She fell silent, and belatedly, Matt realized what a jackass thing that was to say. Once he'd adamantly insisted that marriage would never be in his future. He could still remember the devastated look on her face. Of course, that was long ago. Things had changed for both of them. He was reading too much into her silence.

"How about we pick up some ice cream on the way home? Would Tasha like that?" he asked.

"If you're trying to encourage her, that would work. But I don't want her to have any sugar this late."

"Is this crush thing going to be a problem when your parents get here?"

"No. Little girls worship their daddies all the time."

"Yeah, I guess," he said, veering the car onto her street, uneasy at the melancholy tone of her voice.

Tasha's father had opted out of being a part of her life, and that hurt Lexy. This had nothing to do with him, he reminded himself.

"Let me go on ahead," Lexy said as he started to slow down. "Tasha should be asleep already, and sometimes she doesn't wake up when I carry her to our room. I'd rather she didn't get excited and stay up late."

"I'll park the car and give you...what? Ten minutes?"

"Five minutes should do it," she said, getting out when he came to a stop and taking the cell phone with her.

He waited until she entered her building before he continued down the street to look for a legal parking place. The sidewalks and alleys were littered with old newspapers, beer cans and pop bottles. They lived in a relatively clean city, and he hadn't had much occasion to visit this part of town that proved the exception. He hated even parking his car here. The fact that Lexy lived here was more than he cared to think about.

But he had thought about it. Probably too often. And that was something he wanted to discuss with her. She wasn't going to like it but, in her own new vernacular—tough.

He found a space a block away and jogged back to her apartment. Glancing at his watch, he figured he'd ended up giving her the ten minutes after all, so he knocked lightly at her door.

She opened it almost immediately, and he saw that she'd changed into a pair of faded jeans and a blue T-shirt. Her hair had been pulled back at the restaurant but now it hung in soft waves to her shoulders. She looked exactly like she had when he'd first met her seven years ago, and his heart did an erratic little jog. Lexy had looked younger than nineteen even then. She still did.

That was why he felt so protective of her, he decided. Why he had this urge to draw her into his arms and hold her, keep her safe, get her away from this neighborhood. Raising a child alone was bad enough. Having to worry about her safety, too, had to be mind numbing. And Lexy looked like a child herself.

"Are you coming in or are you going to stand there?"

He blinked, trying to clear away the fog of memories that shrouded his good sense. "Is she asleep?"

Lexy nodded and stepped aside as he crossed the threshold.

He glanced over his shoulder to watch her turn the knob lock. But she ignored the dead bolt.

Matt frowned. "Aren't you going to secure that?"

She returned his frown, then a slow grin twitched at her lips. "When I have a big, strong man here to protect me?"

"Knock it off, Lexy, this is serious."

She rolled her eyes toward the ceiling before she followed him, ignoring the dead bolt. "Matthew, I've been taking care of myself for a long time. So just—"

she pressed her lips together in frustration as if she were at a loss for words, and tugged at her left ear "—you knock it off."

He grinned suddenly. "That means to stop it." He stared at her, unsure if the look she was giving him was one of confusion or irritation. "Knock it off," he explained, "is like telling someone to stop something."

"I know that."

He lifted a hand, and she reared her head slightly until she realized he'd just meant to touch her ear. Her eyes widened as he pulled gently on her lobe. "I remember that you always used to tug at your ear when you couldn't translate a word."

She stood frozen, her gaze finding and holding his. A soft flowery scent that was her own drifted up to send an arousing memory to his groin, and he tensed.

He had no idea what expression he revealed, but alarm suddenly glittered in her eyes and she stepped out of reach. Then she broke eye contact and turned to secure the dead bolt. "I usually do lock this," she admitted in a voice that was a little too high. "But I was irritated by you telling me what to do."

Matt cleared his throat. Tonight wasn't going to be easy. For more than one reason. "I wasn't trying to tell you what to do."

"Of course you were." She brushed past him, jumping a little when her shoulder hit his chest. She snuggled into the recliner, tucking her legs up under her. "But that isn't your right." Her eyes met his again and she added, "Is it?"

They weren't talking about his pushiness anymore. "No, it isn't."

This time he was first to break eye contact. He settled himself on the uncomfortable pink couch.

"Now that we have that straight," she said, "what did you want to discuss?"

Lexy was different, and he wasn't sure he liked the change in her. In the old days, not only would he have gone unchallenged, but she wouldn't have pushed the issue to the point of having the last word.

Hell. She was right. He had no claims or rights where she was concerned. He'd given them up seven years ago. And that undeniable fact was going to make this discussion more difficult.

He had to simply come out with it. She needed to move out of this rattrap. And he was going to help her. She was a reasonable person. She would see the logic in his suggestion.

"Okay," he said, pressing the crease in his khakis with his thumb and forefinger. Then he dusted some lint near his knee as he mentally rehearsed his opening argument. Hearing her impatient sigh, he glanced up. She was staring at him with a puzzled frown. "Have you got anything to drink?" he asked.

Her frown grew more confused. "You mean?"

"Wine would be terrific, but water will do."

"Water," she said. "But I don't have any bottled kind."

"Tap is fine." He watched her get up and move to the small kitchen. Her T-shirt had gotten caught up in the waistband of her jeans, and the worn, faded denim molded her rear end like a soft leather glove. He got heated just watching her move.

When she turned suddenly, he had to shoot his gaze up to meet hers. She'd obviously noticed and returned his smile with a cool one of her own. "Do you want lemon in it?"

The question sounded more like a threat than an offer, and he wanted to kick himself for acting like a moron. "You remembered," he said.

She withdrew a glass from the cupboard and slammed in on the counter. "Is that a yes?"

"Yeah." He thought it was a compliment, too.

She got their water, then brought their glasses back, handing the one with the lemon in it to him before she returned to the recliner. "You were saying?"

He took a sip of the cool water, glancing at the small chest that served as a coffee table. "Do you have a coaster?"

Her short startled laugh turned wry. "It hardly matters, Matthew."

He eyed the battered piece of furniture. The wood was scarred, the corners dinged and nicked beyond repair. It was pretty pathetic-looking.

This was the perfect introduction to his proposal. He set the glass down, then leaned back and met her eyes. "We need to discuss what you've told your parents."

She gave him a stiff nod.

"What specifically do they know about me? Well, not me, but your husband."

She shrugged. "I described you."

"Meaning?"

"It was easier to keep my facts straight if I had a real person in mind, and I just used you. I told them you were a lawyer and that I'd met you while I was in school."

"Good. That makes it easy." Something nagged at him. "You told them I traveled a lot to account for my absence while they're here. Surely they know a divorce attorney wouldn't need to travel.''

Her eyes grew wide, then she looked away. ''I didn't say you were a divorce attorney.''

''Why not?''

''It doesn't matter. I will be doing the talking. They know only six English words.''

''You think there's something wrong with what I do?''

She hesitated, then shook her head but refused to look at him. Shifting uneasily, she plucked at a loose thread from her shirt seam. It was obvious she thought he was some kind of bottom feeder.

''Lexy?'' Stunned, he sank further back, forgetting the proposal he'd carefully prepared. He was one of the most sought-after divorce attorneys in the city. He'd handled numerous celebrity divorces. He was the envy of his peers. Lexy looked as though she were ashamed, or maybe even disgusted.

What was this about?

Shrugging, she finally brought her face up. ''It can't be a very—'' she shrugged again ''—happy job that you have.'' Her accent creeping in, she said, ''Kind of like an undertaker, yes?''

He snorted. ''No.''

''Keep your voice down or you're going to wake Tasha.''

''I'm not raising my voice,'' he said in a lower tone. ''What are you getting at?''

''You used do such good work for poor people, Matthew. You were happy doing that, remember?''

He nodded grudgingly, knowing she was referring to the ACLU work he'd done in law school—when he'd had the time and not so many social commitments.

"Now it's just so sad," she continued. "All these people who love each other are suddenly breaking apart, and you're *helping* them."

"The point is, they no longer love each other, and when the partnership is dissolved, it's up to me to make sure my client gets his or her half of the assets."

She let out a small sound of distress. "And you don't think this is sad?"

"Not if I get them the lion's share of the kill."

At his satisfied smirk, her brows drew together and she folded her arms. "Explain what that means."

He blinked, not anxious to elaborate. Not to Lexy, anyway. "I'm not going to defend my profession to you."

"Of course not." She lifted her chin. "Because you can't."

"Some people think what I do has enormous value."

His sarcasm didn't faze her. She tilted her head to the side and looked genuinely concerned when she asked, "Are these people unhappy, too?"

"Not when I'm through with their case."

Her forehead creased and she looked as though she were making an earnest attempt to understand. "And what do you get out of it, Matthew?" she asked softly.

Chapter Five

Matthew sat in his office and stared at his paycheck, his foul mood eating a hole in his gut. Last night Lexy had not only distracted him from his campaign to get her to move, but she'd had the gall to ask him what he got out of his job. He had a good mind to send this to her. He could throw in a copy of last year's bonus check, too, as well as the slew of social invitations he'd received just in the past week for all the most desirable events of the season.

And who would have thought it? That Lloyd Monroe's son would have climbed this high up the social and professional ladder by the age of thirty-two? Not that his father was lazy or lacking ability. But he'd been content enough grading seventh-grade math papers and taking odd jobs to feed his wife and seven kids. No one accused him of being ambitious.

Thinking about his family, Matt winced when he remembered that he hadn't told them about his upcoming marriage yet. Of course, he hadn't seen them for more than six months. A couple of Sundays ago he'd meant to make the hour-drive home and surprise them, but a tough case had kept him glued to his desk and time had gotten away from him.

They understood. Most of the time, anyway. His older sister had been pretty ticked when he'd missed his niece's baptism last year, and his nephew's birthday. But they were all proud of his accomplishments.

Unlike Lexy.

Hell, it wasn't as if he'd turned his back on pro bono work. He still took on an occasional charity case. But now his time was more important than when he was in law school. He had greater responsibilities now...to his firm...to his...

He stared again at his paycheck.

It wasn't just the money. His work made him feel...

Tossing the check on a pile of legal briefs, he scrubbed at his eyes. He didn't know how he felt anymore. Except tired. Really tired.

The knock at his door was annoyingly brief before it opened, letting him know who his visitor was even before Brad poked his face in.

"Hey, pal, you ready for lunch?"

"Not today." Matt eased forward in his chair and rested his elbows on his desk. "I'm behind."

"Yeah, I noticed you've been ducking out early lately."

"Seven is hardly early."

"For me it's ungodly late, but for you, unheard of. What gives?"

Matt briefly closed his eyes and pinched the bridge of his nose, hoping to lose the sudden headache pulsing in the center of his forehead. "What have you been hanging around here until seven for?"

"The Jefferson case is not the piece of cake we all thought it would be. In fact, I was going to ask you to look at—"

Matt shook his head. "You're going to have to hit someone else up for help. I'm on overload."

Brad frowned and stepped farther into the room, closing the door behind him. "I don't believe it. Our resident white knight is declining to rush in and save the day."

"Shut up, Brad." Matt opened his center desk drawer, pulled out a file and slammed the drawer shut again without looking up. "Grab me a grilled chicken on whole wheat while you're out, huh? And don't forget to tell them to leave off the mayo this time."

"Yeah, sure," Brad said, not making a move to leave. Instead he planted his lanky body in the chair facing Matt's desk. "What's going on?"

"What do you mean?" He shuffled piles of paper, trying to look busy so that his friend would get the hint and split.

"Are you kidding?" Brad laughed. "You've been grouchy, distracted and a general pain in the ass." He narrowed his eyes. "Does this have anything to do with your visit with Lexy?"

"Nope. I told you she's being cooperative. She's going to sign the papers. No problem."

Brad's sandy-colored brows drew together. "*Going* to sign the papers? As in future tense? As in she hasn't already signed them?" At Matt's unsmiling response, he added, "Oh, man, what happened?"

Matt hadn't planned on telling Brad about the deal he made with Lexy, but he'd be foolish not to let him in on it. He might need his friend's help to cover for his absences while Lexy's parents were here.

Matt sighed and leaned back in his chair. "I'm doing her a favor. Her parents are visiting for two weeks and we're going to pretend we're really married."

Brad's jaw slackened, then he cut loose an earthy four-letter word. "You moving in with her?" he asked, his eyes beginning to light up with amused interest.

"No. Nothing like that. Her parents only speak Hungarian. Lexy will tell them that I'm traveling for most of their visit. I'll probably just have to have a couple of dinners with them."

"I don't get it. Why did she lie to them?"

Matt shrugged and recapped his Mont Blanc pen, keeping his gaze lowered. "She has a daughter. She probably doesn't want them to worry about her raising her as a single mother."

"A daughter?" Brad shook his head in amazement. "Hard to imagine." Then he shrugged. "I don't know why. Lexy has to be all grown up now. I bet she still looks terrific."

"Yeah, she looks pretty good."

Brad fell silent, and when Matt, curious, finally glanced up, he saw his friend studying him with a solemn expression. "How old is the kid?" Brad asked.

"Six, seven, something like that. Are you going to get our sandwiches anytime before dinner?" Matt started shuffling again.

"Did she tell you who the father is?"

"Not exactly. She implied he was some lowlife."

"That doesn't sound like Lexy. She was too smart and discriminating to fall for some weasel."

Matt squirmed. His friend had a good point. But obviously she hadn't been discriminating enough. "Go to lunch, Brad. Lexy and her kid aren't my problems, and I've got work to do."

Brad stood, and relief washed over Matt. "One more thing," Brad said. "You and Lexy..." He trailed off, his face pensive, as if trying to censure his normally colorful way of putting things, which pretty much warned Matt of what was coming. "You ever do the wild thing?"

Matt stared his friend down, refusing to answer a question like that, until Brad finally shrugged and let himself out. The problem was, if anyone knew what was going on and got one look at Tasha, there'd be a lot more questions then that.

He massaged the growing tension in his neck, the same tightness that had kept him tossing and turning for the past three nights.

Because, damn it, he still had a few questions of his own.

LEXY FIGURED she would have to win the lottery in order to pay Mrs. Hershey back for all her unconditional kindness. Especially with all the extra time her finals had just taken. But she supposed she'd have to buy a ticket first, and after spending a small fortune on getting her hair trimmed, something as impractical as a lottery ticket wasn't in her near future.

Although seven dollars probably wasn't really a small fortune, Lexy was used to trimming her own hair and she wasn't quite sure why she'd splurged today. Except her parents were arriving in five days, and...

Okay, so she was seeing Matthew in an hour.

"Mommy, can I take a chocolate Pop-Tart over to Mrs. Hershey's for after dinner?" Tasha asked, her head tilted back as she gazed at Lexy. "She's gonna try and give me grapes for dessert again and that isn't fair."

Lexy stifled a grin. "And why isn't that fair?"

"Everybody knows that dessert isn't supposed to be

healthy," she said in a long-suffering voice. "If it was, nobody would want it."

"I see. Where did you hear that?"

"Libby's father. He sneaks Oreo cookies all the time." Tasha paused, and Lexy braced herself for what she knew was coming next. "Tell me about my father again."

Lexy forced a smile. Tasha was growing up so fast, the explanation Lexy gave her would soon no longer be enough.

"Your father loved you very much. He was sad that he had to go away..." Lexy began, but to her relief, Tasha became distracted by her reflection in the chrome teapot sitting on the stove.

She peered closely at her image, squinting when she couldn't get a good-enough look at the two gold barrettes she'd clipped to her hair. The ornaments were too big for her, but Lexy knew better than to argue with the little tyrant when it came to her fashion statements. Besides, Tasha would only be spending the evening at Mrs. Hershey's, bless the woman's kind heart.

It had almost been a relief when Lexy had finally broken down and told her neighbor what was going on. She'd left out some key details, such as her and Matthew's marital status and the part about Natasha. Mrs. Hershey simply thought Matthew was an old friend doing her this favor. And although Lexy doubted the woman approved of the deception, she understood.

"Here you go." Lexy broke a Pop-Tart in two and sealed half in a baggy.

Tasha tore her attention away from her reflection and frowned. "I can eat a whole one."

''This is enough chocolate. And you have milk with it and not soda. You understand?''

Reluctantly, Tasha nodded.

''Let's go or I'll be late.'' Lexy herded her out of the apartment, grabbing her purse off the kitchen counter along the way.

Mrs. Hershey's door was open, and she was sitting in front of the TV watching a game show. When she saw them, she waved Tasha in. Lexy mouthed a thank-you and hurried down the hall to the stairs.

She still had ten minutes before her bus would get to the corner, but she didn't want to cut it too close and have to run in this heat. As horrid as their building's inefficient air-conditioning system was, it was a blessing compared to the unseasonably warm, humid wind that embraced her as soon as she stepped outside.

A discarded newspaper flew up from the sidewalk and flapped against her bare legs. She shook it free, then looked up and saw Matthew's navy blue BMW across the street. He let down the window and waved to get her attention. As if the expensive sedan didn't stick out like a rose from a stem of thorns.

Both annoyed and pleased, she crossed the street. Immediately he jumped out to open her door.

''We were supposed to meet at the restaurant,'' she said as she slipped into the coolness, the leather seats providing a welcome chill against her bare legs.

''I was in the neighborhood.''

She laughed, not feeling so annoyed anymore. Her hair tended to frizz with too much humidity, and waiting at the bus stop would probably have been enough to make it go crazy. ''I don't believe you for a second, but thank you.''

He closed her door, then climbed behind the wheel.

"Have you thought of another restaurant you'd like to go to? I'd suggested Ernie's Steak House because I knew it would be easy for you to get to, but now that isn't a problem."

She shrugged. "I don't know many."

He let the car idle while he furrowed his brow in concentration. "How about…"

She took advantage of his hesitation to check him out. He looked nice. *Really* nice, although he wasn't dressed much differently than he normally dressed. He had on almost the same style of khaki pants, only these were pleated at the waist. And his navy jacket…

He was watching her watch him. She blinked and looked past him out his side window, and from her peripheral vision, she noticed that he glanced down to see what she'd been looking at.

Well, she couldn't come out and tell him that she'd been looking at the pleats in his pants. Except if she didn't, he'd probably think she'd been looking *there*.

Heat surged to her face. "You'd better choose a restaurant where we won't run into your fiancée," she said, having no idea where that thought had come from.

Guilt.

She stared down at the above-knee hem of her pink floral dress and suddenly wished she hadn't gotten a haircut, or put on the only other dress she owned.

"Amanda is dining at the Indian Hill country club tonight. We won't run into her."

"Oh." Not for the first time, curiosity nagged at Lexy. It shouldn't surprise her that Matthew would marry someone who *dined* at a country club, and it didn't, but…

"Look, I don't want tonight starting off the way the other night ended. Tell me what's wrong."

The reminder shamed Lexy. She'd been rude to him three nights ago. He'd never belittled her waitress job, and even if he knew about her cleaning the school offices, she doubted he'd look down on that, either. For all his faults, Matthew valued a strong work ethic. Yet she'd been critical of his career.

"I'm feeling anxious about my parents," she said. "And I feel bad that you have to sneak around."

"Bad enough to call this off?" He shot her a quick look before giving his attention to the car's side mirror as he pulled out into the street.

She stared at his profile in surprise, then annoyance. "I gave you a chance in the beginning. I was going to sign the papers, anyway. I—"

"You're right. I shouldn't have said that."

"Do you want to call it off?"

He didn't answer. Instead, he appeared to be concentrating on the small green sports car in front of him, and cursed under his breath when the other driver braked without warning, then used no signal to make a turn.

She wrung her hands together. "Matthew?"

"Nah, we don't have to call it off."

Lexy swallowed at the hesitant tone of his voice, waiting for him to say something else. Anything. But he didn't and she sat there silently, unsure whether she should let the subject drop or not. They could make it work. She knew they could, and her parents could return to Hungary without worry.

And Lexy could save face.

"I know where we're going," he said suddenly, a slow smile curving his mouth and erasing her concern.

He made a sharp turn without signaling and the person behind them honked. Amused by the irony of what had just happened, she asked, "Are you going to give me a hint?"

"I just did."

Confused, she studied his profile, her gaze resting on the clean cut of his jaw. He was still smiling slightly in a smug sort of way, and she realized he wasn't going to tell her anything more.

She transferred her attention to their surroundings, trying to figure out where they were when it hit her. They were headed toward their old neighborhood.

With mixed feelings, she took a deep breath. Too many old memories lurked in the shadows of the small cottages that lined the street to the university. They had lived in the third one on the right. Matthew had given her the only bedroom. On the outside, they appeared to be a happily married couple, always prepared for that unannounced Immigration and Naturalization Service visit. Except Matthew had always slept on the couch. Until that last night.

"What's wrong?"

She felt something warm, solid, and she looked down to see one large hand gently cupping her two clasped ones. Disengaging her cramped fingers, she realized she'd been wringing the life out of them.

As soon as she pulled one hand free, Matthew returned his to the steering wheel. "Why are you so nervous?" he asked without looking at her.

It had been a long time since a man touched her like that, and she felt so horribly needy all of a sudden that it frightened her to death. What was so pathetic was that it hadn't even been much of a touch.

But it *was* Matthew.

And they were going back to the old neighborhood where it had all started, and she didn't think she could bear it.

"Stop the car," she said.

"What?" He shot her a puzzled look. "Here?"

She nodded, trying to swallow the lump of panic lodged in her throat.

"Here?" he repeated.

Her gaze locked on a flashing red vacancy sign. "There."

Matthew put on the brakes and narrowly missed the parking lot entrance before steering them to a spot under the sign. His stunned gaze drew to the orange neon letters above it that read Stay Awhile Motel.

MATT OPENED the door and let Lexy precede him into the motel lobby. He was definitely going to let her do the talking. Not that she was making much sense. But big-shot lawyer and master of legalese that he was, he couldn't form a single coherent sentence right now if his life depended on it.

The twenty-something woman behind the desk glanced up and stopped chomping her gum. A college kid, he guessed. They were near enough to their old campus that the next four blocks would be crawling with rabid packs of know-it-alls.

"Can I help you?" the woman asked, peering at them through oversize red glasses.

Lexy cleared her throat. "We'd like to see a room, please."

Matt let out a stream of air, then smiled briefly when the clerk's probing gaze swept him. Maybe he should have waited in the car.

"Do you want to *see* a room, or rent one?" the woman asked.

"We'd like to *see* one first," Lexy said primly. "But I'm more interested in your beds. So if you have different sizes and room setups, I'd like to see them all."

The other woman's eyes widened a fraction, and she chewed once, twice, before letting her gaze wander back to Matthew.

Yup, he thought, stuffing his hands into his pockets and slowly diverting his attention to the chips in the ceiling, the cobweb in the right top corner, the plain white walls...he should have stayed in the car.

"Sure," the clerk said, "I have about three different types I can show you."

She ducked to get something from under the counter, and when Matt heard keys rattling he risked a look in her direction. Her name tag read Denise.

"We have to access the rooms from outside," she said, heading toward the door. "So if you'll follow me..."

Lexy had barely glanced at him since leaving the car, and she refused to look at him now. For a minute he thought he'd known what she was doing, but now he wasn't so sure. She looked nervous and flushed and even a little unsteady. As she followed Denise out the door, she nearly tripped on the slightly raised threshold.

He put out a hand to cup her waist, and she sent a menacing glare over her shoulder worthy of any prosecutor. Immediately he backed off and she continued walking.

Funny, he didn't remember Lexy as moody, but he

was being treated to a full spectrum of emotion now. Strange. Very strange.

"This is a double-double room," Denise said, opening the first door, then sticking her arm in to flip on a light.

That her arm came back in one piece Matthew took as a good sign. The entire place was a dump, from the faded exterior yellow walls to the chipped orange trim framing smudged windows.

Lexy went in ahead of everyone, taking slow, gingerly steps. The clerk moved back to let Matthew go in after Lexy. He wasn't sure he wanted to, but he summoned his lagging courage and followed, hoping Lexy wouldn't bite his head off just because he was close enough for her to do so.

The room was dingy and dark even with the soft glow of the bedside lamp. The comforters were muddy brown, the walls white…maybe. The place gave him the willies.

Lexy sighed. "We need a bigger bed." She turned and blinked at the woman. "Do you have one?"

"Sure." A small, knowing smile tugged at Denise's lips as they filed out and she locked the door.

The next room was no better. Although Matt had to admit this one looked clean enough, the drab olive-green decor made it unappealing. It did, however, boast a king-size bed.

Denise arched her brows first at Lexy, then at him. "How about this?"

"Don't ask me," he said. "Ask my wife."

Chapter Six

He hadn't meant to say that. And Lexy certainly hadn't expected it either, judging by the size of her eyes. The way she was looking at him reminded him of one of those big-eyed little kids in paintings that were popular when he was still arguing over whether he could ride his skateboard to school.

"Oh, no." Denise craned her neck to look out the window. "Someone else just pulled up." She let go of the curtain, then squinted at them, as if sizing them up. "I guess it'll be okay to leave you here while I go see what they want."

Then she scooted out the door before either Matt or Lexy could say a word.

Lexy switched her gaze from the empty doorway to him. "I can't believe you called me your wife."

He shrugged. What was he supposed to say? Technically, she still was. Although the word had merely slipped out when he'd seen the suggestive look on the clerk's face. He'd expected her next question to be whether they wanted the room for one hour or two. Not that he gave a rat's behind what the young woman thought, but Lexy would.

"Just trying to get in character," he said, feeling

odd all of a sudden, as if the mere act of saying the word *wife* had altered the inside of his mouth.

But Lexy legally was his wife, he thought again, and his mouth got even drier.

"Oh." Abruptly she turned from him, and he wondered what in his expression caused her obvious unease. "I guess we should try the bed."

Matt reared back his head. Was she joking?

Oblivious to his dazed reaction, she lowered herself to the edge of the mattress and bounced slightly. She ran her gaze the length of the bed, then over his face, her eyebrows drawing together in a small frown. "How tall are you?"

"Uh, six-one."

"Hmmm." Her gaze returned to the bed.

"Hey, uh, Lexy..." He rubbed the side of his neck, restless suddenly, as he briefly considered how to word his thoughts.

She waited patiently, her eyes wide and questioning...her breasts jiggling when she gave another small bounce.

He took a quick breath. "This little stop. It's a... I'm thinking you're considering this motel for your parents?"

She smiled. "Of course, Matthew." She bounced again. "What do you think?"

His gaze automatically drew to her breasts. "That we need to get the hell out of here," he muttered under his breath, and left the room, heading for the car.

Lexy appeared behind him in a flash. "I didn't hear you," she said, her eyes dark with concern. "Is something wrong, Matthew? You look awful."

"We're going to be late for dinner."

"But I wanted you to try the bed. My father is six-five and sometimes has trouble with mattresses being too short.''

Great. He rubbed his eyes. The guy was probably going to kick the crap out of him when he found out what Matt had done to his daughter.

"Can we discuss this at dinner, Lexy?"

She gave him an odd look. "But we're here now."

They were standing in the middle of the small parking lot, and it was starting to get dark. Shadows eclipsed her face, distorting her expression. He didn't want to tell her that they couldn't put her parents in this fleabag motel. She was going to take offense at his objection, accuse him of being a snob, even though he knew she'd never choose a place like this, either, if money weren't an issue.

He held out a hand. "Lexy, let's go have a nice dinner and we'll discuss everything then."

She opened her mouth to argue, but closed it again without saying a word as she accepted his hand.

Matt squeezed gently, then drew her to him. Her upturned face was clouded with mild confusion. But he saw trust there, too. Lexy had always done that. She'd trusted him, as misguided as that faith had proved to be.

Resolutely ignoring his very masculine response to her soft curves, he gave her a companionable hug, then steered them toward the car. This time he wouldn't let her down.

LEXY SOMEHOW thought men were supposed to mellow with age, become less confusing. At least, that's what her mother had taught her. Matthew didn't follow the rules. He totally baffled her. Of course, he was only thirty-two. He still had time. But he wouldn't be mellowing with her. He was going to marry someone named Amanda.

That hurt, even though she knew it shouldn't. She stared at the cherry floating in her soda and reminded herself not to make too much of his bringing her here. It was close to her apartment and there was little chance of them running into anyone he knew. That was all.

"You're not thinking of having another one," Matthew said, his tone disbelieving as he narrowed his gaze at her cherry soda.

She eyed the spoon poised over his half-eaten strawberry sundae. "A double bacon cheeseburger, fries, a vanilla shake and that mound of sugar." She made a face. "Don't criticize me."

"Wouldn't dream of it, honey." He dropped the spoon, letting it clang into the glass dish, and pushed the remaining ice cream away. "Now that you've pointed out how much junk I've put into my system, I'm not feeling so hot."

She'd leaned forward a little to hear him. The restaurant was quickly filling up with college kids, laughing and talking over music that was far too loud for her old-lady ears. She thought he'd called her "honey," although she knew it meant nothing. It was just that he'd never used the term with her before, and for some reason it made her feel a little strange.

"Were you surprised we came here?" he asked.

"I was unsure at first, but then I figured out where we were going."

He studied her in silence for a moment, his expression growing more somber. "Was this a bad idea?"

"Of course not." She picked up her Cherry Coke and sipped. It was her second one, and the syrupy sweetness was beginning to lose its charm. Setting the glass down again, she shrugged.

He nodded. "We had some good times here with Brad and Mark and Caroline."

She laid her head back against the postered wall and gazed at the overhead ceiling fan, letting the memories filter through her head. Recollections had been slipping in and out of her thoughts all evening, most of them surprisingly pleasant. She grinned. "How is Brad? Did he ever pass the—" She couldn't remember the term. "That lawyer's exam?"

"The bar exam? Not until the second try." Matthew immediately got out his wallet when the waitress put the check down, and handed her a charge card without looking at the total.

Someday, Lexy promised herself, she'd be able to do that. She and Tasha would treat themselves to a real sit-down restaurant and they'd order anything but fries or burgers or chicken nuggets. "Do you see him much?"

"Every day. He works for the same law firm I do."

Delighted initially with the news, Lexy suddenly felt a jolt of jealous longing. As much as she'd wanted to be part of their crowd, she never really was one of them. She'd been too young, too shy. They'd only let her hang around because she'd bought and paid for Matthew's attention. "What about Mark and Caroline?"

"They ended up getting married." Matthew was watching her with unnerving intensity, then he shrugged and idly glanced away. "I only see them occasionally."

She didn't believe him. Not that it mattered how often he saw his law school friends. But she was upset that he seemed to have read her conflicted emotions and felt he had to temper their conversation.

Straightening, she said, "Let's get back to the reason for this dinner."

"Okay," he said. "Let's review the timeline. Your parents arrive in three days. I'm going with you to pick them up at the airport." He paused. "Unless you want to borrow my car and pick them up by yourself."

"I don't know how to drive."

"You're kidding?"

She made a face. "What difference does it make? I've never owned a car."

"But you didn't even learn?"

"Who was going to teach me?" she asked, and when she saw guilt and pity collide in his face, she tensed. The fact the he would feel any guilt at all was nonsense. Their arrangement had been pure business. He'd reminded her of that often enough.

"How are you going to show your parents around?"

"Cabs, buses. We'll be fine."

"Yeah, but—"

"Matthew," she said softly, her smile wry. "My parents won't think anything of it. They aren't rich people and they live a different life-style than most Americans. My father has owned only one car and he's kept it for twenty years now."

He drummed two fingers on the table, his sigh filling the space between them. "Guess I really don't know that much about you."

Thank goodness. He was going to be more than a little surprised when he met her parents. Shifting into a more comfortable position, she wondered if now was the time to warn him. She shrugged. "It wasn't necessary."

"Right," he said just as the waitress returned with the charge slip and left it on the table. He picked up the pen. "About the transportation problem, won't they wonder why I haven't bought you a car?" He leaned back, his expression a strange mixture of irritation and mockery. "I mean, here you told them I was this wonderful guy."

Lexy gazed at him in astonishment. It was obvious he felt slighted somehow. "I'm not worried. That isn't the problem, it's—" She stopped herself from revealing more of her fears than she'd intended.

"The apartment," he said, finishing for her.

Her shoulders sagged and she nodded. The problem was obvious. She didn't know why she was so touchy about it.

"I've been thinking about that, too," he said, carefully watching her reaction. "And I think I've found a solution. I have this—"

"No," she said quickly. "I won't impose on you like that. We can't use your home."

"God, no." Instant shock drained the blood from his face. "I mean..." He rubbed his jaw, scratched the side of his neck, adjusted his collar. "That wouldn't work."

Speechless with embarrassment, Lexy watched him snatch the charge slip and scribble his name across the bottom. She couldn't believe she'd blurted that out. Could she have jumped to a more foolish conclusion?

"It's not that I don't want to make the offer," he said, finally looking up. His reluctant eyes met her mortified ones. "It would simply be too difficult to keep this situation from Amanda, and—"

"You don't have to explain. Please." She took a shaky breath. "I don't know what I was thinking."

He reached across the table for her fisted hand, and she let him cup his palm around it. "Normally, that would have been a logical solution, so don't worry about it. Besides, my place isn't designed for a kid."

She narrowed her eyes. "Natasha has perfect manners. She would not disrupt your things."

"Don't get hot under the collar. I don't know that much about kids."

She withdrew her hand from his. Although she didn't quite understand the phrase he'd used, she didn't like his tone. "That's right. You don't know anything about children. So you leave my daughter to me."

He let out a grunt of surprise. "When did this get personal? I meant nothing against Natasha."

Reaching for her purse, she started to push back her chair and rise. She was surprised he even remembered her daughter's name. Matthew had made it clear early on that children had no place in his future.

"Come on, Lexy. What are you getting so ticked off for? You haven't even heard my plan."

"I have one of my own, thank you."

"Then you wanna let me in on it?" he asked dryly, and she paused, then sank back down again.

"Of course. I'm going to tell them we are remodeling our house and we are temporarily living in my apartment. I mean, they'll think it's ours, of course."

He stared at her as if she'd gone crazy. "They won't believe that."

"Yes, they will, and that story goes along perfectly with why they have to stay in a motel."

"If anything, we'd be staying at the motel with

them, and not in a—'' He waved a hand through the air.

"In a place like mine?"

He met her gaze squarely. "Exactly."

She flinched.

"I don't want to hurt your feelings, Lexy, but I'm trying to help and you're making things difficult. Let's be realistic and tackle this problem together."

Lexy stared at the thumbnail she'd torn while cleaning the school offices yesterday. *Sure, Matthew, be logical and emotionless and indifferent. You're so good at it.*

"Agreed?" he asked.

Looking up, she nodded. "What's your plan?"

"I have a friend who owns a building where they rent corporate apartments by the week or month. There are one, two or three bedrooms, totally furnished. All you'd have to do is take some clothes with you. I'll ask him if he has a two-bedroom available."

"But, Matthew, if we get the larger one, my parents could stay with me and not in a motel," she said, excited at the prospect. For all the worry their visit was causing her, she was anxious to see them.

He frowned. "No, because then they would expect me to be sleeping there the nights I'm supposed to be in town."

"Oh."

"Better to keep it simple."

Simple? She wanted to laugh. "Umm, your friend, how much does he charge?"

"This will be a freebie, I promise you. I do a lot of legal work for him at no charge."

Relieved, she wasn't going to argue. "I will admit, this is a good plan, Matthew. My parents are...maybe a little eccentric, but they wouldn't like my apartment much.''

At his sudden guarded expression, she bit her lip. She'd purposely searched her English dictionary for the best word to describe her parents and not sound so alarming. She'd discovered *eccentric* two nights ago. Maybe she didn't truly understand the word's meaning.

She tugged at her ear. ''Matthew? You look... worried.''

His eyebrows were drawn together. ''I was just thinking. We'll have to fill out a calendar. Maybe tape one up somewhere in the apartment showing the days I'm supposed to be out of town. That way you won't get confused. We can even mark it for a couple of extra months just to make it look good.'' At her bewildered frown, he added, ''So it doesn't look like we've done it only for their visit.''

Understanding dawned, and she nodded. He was very good at this deception business, she thought, but chose not to voice her opinion. He would probably take it wrong.

''And about that roadside motel we stopped at,'' he said, narrowing his gaze in disapproval. ''I'm sure we can do better than that.''

She studied her napkin in private agreement. But she wasn't about to admit that she'd asked him to stop in sheer panic, that she'd been frightened over her possible reaction to their old haunt. ''I will look at a couple of places before work tomorrow.''

He pursed his lips. ''What are you going to do about work while they're here?''

''I have vacation time coming. I already settled it with my boss.''

"Okay. What else do we need to do?" he asked. "I'm going to be tied up with a case for the next couple of days. Have you figured out how you'll handle Tasha?"

"She only knows a few Hungarian words. I've been referring to you as Popo and so has she. It's a name I called my father when I was a child. She believes it's just a nickname. Of course my parents will think…" A tightness in her chest startled her. This pretense was hitting too close to home. "Well, you know what they'll think. But don't worry, they won't see the two of you together much."

"What about dinner? Won't she come with us when we take them out?"

Lexy sighed with frustration at having forgotten something so obvious. This wasn't going to work. How had she ever thought it would?

Apparently he sensed her despair and gave her a reassuring smile. "Look, after my case is over, I'll spend the two evenings with her before they get here so she can get used to me, and when the time comes for family dinner out, we'll go to one of those places for kids." He waved a dismissive hand. "You know the kind I mean. Chuck E. Cheese or something like that. That way she'll be too distracted to worry about me."

"You would do that?"

"Sure. Why not?"

Clearly he hadn't been to a Chuck E. Cheese yet. But he had to know how spirited a children-oriented restaurant was and she was impressed that he was willing to do that. The two nights with Tasha still made her nervous, though. She didn't want him having too much one-on-one contact with her daughter.

"What about Amanda?" she asked. "How are you going to explain all those evenings away from her?"

His startled reaction gave her pause, and puzzled, she added, "I meant your fiancée. I thought that was her name."

"It is, but she won't miss my presence, believe me."

"Oh." Lexy tried to keep the surprised curiosity off her face, but it was obvious she failed.

He narrowed his eyes at her. "Amanda and I have an understanding. Our relationship may not be right for everyone, but it suits us perfectly. Besides, she has her hobbies."

The lengthy personal explanation was uncharacteristic of him. And when he angrily shoved the signed charge voucher to the edge of the table, she wondered if he regretted volunteering the information.

"I just wouldn't want you to get in trouble with her," she said quietly.

"Anything else we need to discuss?"

"I don't think so." Obviously the current topic was off limits.

"Good." He removed his napkin from his lap and stood. "If I think of anything else, I'll call you."

"Or we can discuss it when you come and see Tasha." She slung her purse strap over her shoulder and stood, too. With his abrupt behavior, she hesitated to push, but... "This is my only night off. But I'd like to be there when you see Tasha."

He seemed vaguely curious, but not too put off by her request. "So, you're saying you want me to wait until you get home from work? Won't that be too late for her to stay up?"

Lexy started for the door. Every table was full of

college kids, most of them crowding into the aisles on extra chairs, and she had to do some fancy maneuvering to get to a spot near the door where she could turn and answer him.

By then his expression was more than curious, it was irritated. "I'm sorry," she said, "I wasn't trying to be rude. It's just so loud in there."

"I know." He gestured toward the door. "The noise level was getting to me, too."

Oh, my, he was going to *love* Chuck E. Cheese. She slid him a sidelong look and was relieved to see the annoyance gone from his face.

Her automatic relief grated on her.

Old memories of trying to appease Matthew, of trying to keep him happy, being so careful that she didn't do anything to upset him crashed down on her. Of course, she'd been younger then, shy and feeling terribly alone, and she'd long since promised herself she would never sacrifice her own wants and needs to make Matthew or any man happy.

That's why the sudden relief bothered her. But he was doing her a favor, too, and she couldn't afford to make him angry, either.

She sighed at the complexity of human relationships, especially that of the male-female variety. Maybe it wasn't so bad being single.

"What was that big sigh for?" Matthew asked with a smile in his voice. He brought a comforting arm up to circle her shoulders, his beautiful blue eyes closing in and stirring up a deeply buried neediness, and she just felt like socking him.

His body was warm and solid, and his scent both mysterious and expensive. Sweet strawberry breath danced across her heated cheek.

He was too attractive, too confusing, too…too…

He made her feel drunk, off balance, weak in her knees. It was a scary feeling and she pulled away from him.

Luckily, they had arrived at the car and he didn't seem to notice her unease. He simply unlocked the passenger door and opened it for her.

Quickly she got inside without looking at him. To have done so would have put their eyes too close, their lips in kissing distance. The act would have been more than foolish, it would have been suicidal.

"What time's your curfew?" he asked as he reversed the car out of the narrow parking lot and onto the street.

Lexy started to relax again. She liked it when he teased her. His voice would dip a little lower than usual, and he'd eventually dart her a covert look to see if he'd made her smile.

"Hey." She sat up straighter. "Why don't we go back and pick Tasha up for ice cream? She would be so thrilled."

He groaned.

"You were going to spend some time with her, anyway," she pointed out, miffed at his reaction. "And of course, I'll pay."

"How can you possibly think about eating so soon?"

"Oh." She rubbed her left arm, smarting because she'd misjudged him. "I didn't mean for *us* to have more ice cream. Just Tasha. She hasn't had sugar today, and chocolate swirl in a cone will win her over forever."

"Let's go."

"And don't say anything about her hair."

"Why would I do that?" He slanted her a look before focusing on the stream of red taillights ahead of them.

"Sometimes she gets too creative with her colored bows and clips."

"A walking Christmas tree, huh?"

"Matthew," she warned, drawing his name out. "She won't know you're teasing."

He grinned. "I won't say a word."

Lexy snuggled into the deep leather seat and smiled, too. For several miles, comfortable silence enfolded them like a favorite wool coat until Matthew slipped a CD into the player and a soft, soothing instrumental filled the air around them.

Everything was going to be okay, she thought, feeling so content and drowsy that it seemed like only seconds later when they turned onto her street.

The city bus she should have taken pulled away from its stop, and she smiled again because tonight she was feeling lazy and spoiled. In front of her apartment building, a taxi cab sat in the only available spot, so Matthew lingered two car lengths away.

Her apartment building door opened and two couples strolled toward the cab.

Lexy blinked, incredulous over what she thought she saw, and strained for a better look.

She let out a squeal of alarm and slid to the floor of the car.

Chapter Seven

Matt stared at the top of Lexy's head. "What the hell is going on? What are you doing down there?"

She wouldn't look up. She scrunched down lower until her face was practically between her knees. Flapping a hand wildly, she said, "Go, Matthew, just drive."

"Can't you tell me—"

She growled. "No. Drive."

"Okay." As he shifted the car from Neutral to Drive, he scanned the sidewalk to discover what had spooked her. Two women were getting into a cab while their escorts waited on the side. The men were both big, dark and as broad as a couple of skyscrapers. One of them had on strange clothes, a kind of studded vest and voluminous black pants. Other than their size, they didn't look particularly threatening.

Besides an elderly lady pushing a grocery cart just past Lexy's building, there wasn't another soul to be seen. Nor nothing out of the ordinary.

"The car isn't moving," Lexy said, her voice muffled from her crunched position. "Why aren't we moving?"

Matt stepped on the accelerator. "Any place in particular, Your Highness?"

"Around the block. No, keep going until you hit Patsy's."

"You want to give me a hint who this Patsy is?"

"It's an all-night diner up two blocks on the right." She shifted, grunting when she didn't have enough room to change positions.

"Are you going to tell me what's so interesting down there?"

"Why are we stopping?" she asked, tilting her head to the side, her anxious gaze flicking over him.

At her genuine look of fear, he discarded the sarcastic retort he'd already formed. "Red light."

"Where's the taxi?"

"The one that was in front of your apartment?" he asked while checking the rearview mirror. "It just turned left on the street behind us."

"Okay. Just keep going toward Patsy's for now." She pulled her purse off the seat and started rummaging through it with frantic jerks.

"We're not going anywhere until you tell me what's going on," he said at the same time someone behind them blared their horn when the light changed to green.

"Oh, Matthew, please don't call attention to us," she said, her eyes widening on him.

He wasn't sure if it was the panic forcing out her accent or the way her brown eyes had grown alarmingly glassy, but he did as she asked without another word. A minute later, the dingy diner came into view under a lighted green sign with a missing *A*.

"You can come up now. We're here." He glanced around, not liking the neighborhood, or the way the sidewalk was deserted except for two grungy-looking kids on the corner sharing a cigarette. Or worse.

He turned the car off, anyway, and waited for her to emerge from her crouched position.

"Is there anyone around?" she asked.

Matt rubbed his eyes, then stared at the boys. One kid's baggy pants had slipped so far down he'd trip over his next step. "No one to worry about."

Tentatively, she bobbed her head up. As she struggled to get her bottom back on the seat, she cringed with the effort and massaged the top of one thigh.

"Cramps?"

"It's okay," she said, and quickly glanced around, her gaze lingering on the two boys, then sweeping the street behind them.

"I can't wait to hear this, but I can wait long enough to forget this place," he said, inclining his head toward the diner. "We're not going in there."

She glared at him for a second, then returned to digging through her purse until she withdrew the cell phone he'd given her. "I wouldn't use this unless it was an emergency," she said as she started dialing.

He threw up a hand. "We're finally getting somewhere. What's the damn emergency?"

"Those people—in front of my apartment?" she said as she brought the phone to her mouth. "They're my parents."

He reared back his head. "But they—"

"Mrs. Hershey?" Lexy started to slip into Hungarian, stopped, briefly closed her eyes and took a deep, audible breath. "I know," she said in accented English. "I saw them. What did you tell them?" She paused as she listened, her free hand picking furiously at the seam of her dress. "Do you know where they went?"

He took her hand to still its frantic fidgeting. Her skin was ice cold, and she let him sandwich her fingers between his warm palms. This was about all the support he could offer at the moment. He had no idea what the hell they were going to do about this unexpected turn of events.

Tomorrow was the start of a grueling, high-profile case. He had every hope of wrapping it up in two days because he had an ace up his sleeve not even his client knew about, but the coup would take all of his time and concentration.

"No, Mrs. Hershey. No, of course not. Please, no, you did the right thing." Lexy was squeezing the life out of his left hand. "Thank you."

She released him to cut the connection on the cell phone. He missed her touch but not the nails digging into his thumb. "Well…"

She let out a shaky laugh. "We don't have to worry about a motel now. Mrs. Hershey found them one in the phone book."

"Why are they here already?"

"I don't know. Mrs. Hershey heard them knocking on my door and went to see who it was and ended up telling them that I was out of town tonight."

"And Tasha?"

She shook her head. "Already asleep. They didn't know she was there."

He drove a hand through his hair. For someone normally quick on his feet, his brain was annoyingly blank. "Okay, good, we have time to come up with another plan."

Her nod was unenthusiastic.

"Come on, Lexy." He slipped a hand around her neck to cup her nape. "This is just a minor setback."

She turned large, anxious eyes on him. A streetlight shining into the car illuminated a suspicious sheen of moisture. "I know. I'm okay, really."

Making a decision, he turned the key in the ignition. "We're going back to my place. You'll be too jumpy in your apartment to discuss anything, and I sure as hell am not going to sit in old Patsy's diner and keep looking over my shoulder."

"Fine," she said, turning her face to look straight ahead.

But her tone told him another story. This wasn't fine. She was irritated about something. Or maybe she was just edgy. Or then again, she'd probably taken offense at his remark about the diner. This was her neighborhood, after all.

Too bad. They had more important things to worry about. And she did live in a crummy part of town. No getting around that. Which reminded him that he hadn't wanted Lexy to know where he lived.

Not because he didn't trust her or expected her to show up on his doorstep uninvited. But the disparity between their two places was almost embarrassing. Too late now.

He took a deep breath and turned the car toward the freeway. When it was clear that they would be heading out of the city, Lexy straightened and asked, "Where *do* you live?"

"Only about fifteen minutes away. Do you need to call Mrs. Hershey again?"

"She suggested that I stay away for another hour or two, so she's not expecting me. Although she doesn't think they'll come back tonight. They believed that we were both out of town.''

As soon as she said that, something that had been vaguely gnawing at Matt finally materialized for him and he slanted her a curious look. ''Does Mrs. Hershey speak Hungarian?''

Lexy's slumped back in her seat and raised a hand to her forehead. ''No.''

He didn't like the way she winced or the way her hand shook, but he was forced to return his attention to the road and a steady string of cars merging into their lane from an on-ramp.

''Lexy?'' He darted her another look. ''Help me out here, Lex. What am I missing?''

''My brother came, too.''

''Your brother,'' he repeated because she had mumbled, and because he was hoping he'd heard incorrectly. ''As in the only one in your family who speaks English?''

''Yes,'' she snapped.

''Great.'' He thought back for a moment. ''Who was the fourth person?''

''My sister.''

He snorted. ''Is there anyone in your family who didn't come to visit?''

''Danica doesn't know English. She isn't the problem.'' Lexy laid her head back and massaged her left temple.

Matt let out a pithy four-letter word his mother had once grounded him a week for using.

Lexy groaned. ''I'm going to have to tell them the truth.''

To agree with her was almost more temptation than Matt could resist. Until he saw the way her lower lip trembled, the way she clutched her stomach with her other hand.

He steered them off the freeway, deciding to say nothing in haste as he navigated the car through the upscale neighborhood where he'd bought a house last year. The place had really been too big for him, but he'd regarded it as an investment at the time, so that Uncle Sam couldn't dig his hand too deeply into Matt's pockets.

And now, of course, he was marrying Amanda and needed the space.

Recalling his fiancée, and how he hadn't told her a damn thing yet, he let out another earthy word. He sighed. "We'll figure this out."

She shook her head. "I'll just tell them the truth."

He turned into his short driveway and pressed the garage door opener on his visor. While he waited for the door to sweep up, he used the opportunity to study Lexy's profile.

She lifted her chin slightly, and her eyes were wide open as she stared straight ahead.

Was she serious? Was she really considering telling them? Or was she testing him? Or maybe just waiting for him to reassure her that everything would be all right. Hell, he didn't know.

It was dark and her face had been cast in shadows. Maybe he'd imagined that she was more upset than she really was. Maybe she'd finally seen reason and understood the foolishness of trying to pull off this charade.

Maybe he was off the hook.

He pulled the car into the garage and got out to flip on the light switch. As soon as Lexy got out and the garage light illuminated her face, he realized how troubled she really felt.

Her cheeks were pale, her mouth turned down at the corners, her eyes a dull brown. She showed no curiosity in her surroundings but merely rounded the rear of the car and, like a zombie, followed him up the two steps into the kitchen.

Fortunately for him, his housekeeper, Gertrude, had come this morning. The counters were spotless, the appliances gleaming. And he knew he could count on his refrigerator having been well stocked.

"Would you like a beer or some wine?" he asked while shrugging out of his blazer. He also had soft drinks, but he figured she'd want something stronger.

"A triple shot of whiskey."

He smiled. "One white wine coming up."

"I wonder if I should call Mrs. Hershey."

"The phone is right there." He gestured with his chin toward the far wall as he brought down two wineglasses from the cupboard. "Ask her which motel she sent them to."

"I'm not calling." She smoothed her hands down her dress. "It's late and I'll only wake Tasha. She'll wonder where I am, and…I've already caused Mrs. Hershey enough trouble."

"How?" His gaze narrowed in suspicion. For whatever reason, he had the feeling she was still holding something back.

"She had to lie for me, Matthew. That wasn't fair."

He turned so she wouldn't see his mouth curve. It obviously hadn't bothered her to ask him to lie. "Don't start feeling sorry for yourself. That won't get us anywhere."

She gave him a dirty look. "I am not feeling sorry

for myself. I'm feeling guilty.'' She closed her mouth, opened it again, then promptly clamped it closed and started pacing the length of the kitchen.

It didn't take a Ph.D. in psychology to know what she wanted to say. And if she thought guilt was foreign to him, she was nuts.

"Here." He handed her a glass. "Let's go into the living room."

"You think I'm wrong, don't you?" she asked, accepting the wine and catching his gaze.

"It doesn't matter what I think."

She sniffed and preceded him as if she knew where she was going. "I guess not."

He followed her through the swinging door. She stopped immediately on the other side and he froze to keep from running her over.

"I'm really in trouble," she said, slowly shaking her head but not looking at him.

He set his wine on the glass dining room table, then placing his hands on her shoulders, turned her to face him. Her eyes were dark and troubled. And close. Very close. He took the glass from her hands and set it next to his, then returned his hand to her shoulder.

She didn't try to move or look away. She simply stared at him, waiting for him to say something.

"Let's be optimistic. Them showing up like this could work in our favor."

"How?" Her skeptical frown produced a tiny dimple near the lower corner of her mouth, momentarily distracting him. She had a great mouth. Her smile had been one of the first things he'd noticed about her. "Matthew?"

"Yeah..." He let his palms slide down her arms, her skin feeling warm and smooth under his. When his hands reached hers, he tugged her toward the living room. Standing there so close to her, inhaling her beguiling scent, wasn't smart. The softness in her eyes, the way she took little nibbles at her lower lip was making his thought process fuzzy.

After ushering her to the sofa, he got her wine and set it beside her on a monogrammed coaster from a set Amanda had given him for a housewarming gift.

Lexy settled back against the snow-white cushions and flicked a glance around the room. "This is beautiful, Matthew."

"Yeah." His impatient gaze darted to the original pewter-and-brass sculpture sitting on a marble pedestal in the corner, the avant-garde set of candleholders adorning the mantel. He knew it was an attractive room. But Amanda's decorator had put it together and somehow Matt had never bonded with it.

When he brought his gaze back to Lexy's anxious face, he found his original train of thought had gotten derailed.

"You were telling me why this may be a good thing?" she prompted, and took a small sip of her wine.

He inhaled a gulp of his. "Since your family is here early and you weren't expecting them yet, we'll have less to account for." He shrugged at her perplexed look. "You can say that I'm out of town, that I was trying to get my work tied up before their arrival. Maybe we can stretch that excuse out for a week."

Her expression fell before she tried to hide it by taking another small sip.

"What? I think that would work out great. It sure makes things easy for me," he said, but as soon as the words were out of his mouth, he understood her crestfallen look. "And you, too," he said. "This new scenario creates less contact between Tasha and me."

"You're right," she said without conviction.

"You think I'm going to desert you," he said, and she quickly dropped her gaze to her knees.

"I didn't say that."

She didn't have to. History had proved his capacity for jerkhood in that area. "We need to get moving," he said, and rose to get the portable phone. "I'm calling my friend to arrange for the apartment we discussed at dinner. Then we're going back to your place to pack some things to take over there. We'll have to wake Tasha and have a little talk with her."

Lexy's eyes had widened as she watched him pick up the phone and press the numbers. Earlier, she looked as though she'd been in mild shock, and whether or not she took exception to his take-charge style now, he didn't know. But time was closing in. Besides, he had that big case tomorrow and...

"Tom?" Matt's turned his attention to the phone. "I know it's late but I need a favor. Summit Manor—do you have a two-bedroom unit available for two weeks?"

As Matt listened to his friend's response, his eyes found Lexy's and her worried look told him he'd not hidden his frustration over his friend's news well.

"No problem," he said, and hung up the receiver.

"What?"

"He won't have anything for a week."

She nodded, looking lost, defeated, and she shrugged. "There's still the motel."

He sighed, stretching his neck to the side, trying like hell to ease the tension that threatened to give him an all-night headache. His desk in the next room was covered with depositions and enough paperwork to keep him up half the night preparing for his case. This unexpected irritation was the last thing he needed.

He met Lexy's eyes, and her crushed look went right through him. "You'll stay here." He was going to regret this. Hell, he already regretted it. "Finish your wine, then we'll go get some of your things."

Wordlessly she watched him pace the room a couple of times. He had two guest bedrooms. Lexy could take one and Tasha could have the other, except he wasn't sure if the second one even had a bed. Hell, he couldn't remember. He doubted he'd been in there since he'd bought the house. But there was a leather couch in his study and he supposed they could always move it into the room if necessary.

There were also two and a half bathrooms. He was relatively sure of that fact...or maybe... Stopping, he frowned. "We probably should go take a quick tour."

He brought his attention back to Lexy and saw that her lips had started to curve. Calmly she set down her wineglass, rose from her seat and started walking toward him.

"It's that way," he said, gesturing toward the hall behind her.

Ignoring him, she continued to advance, and he had the absurd desire to back up and run like hell.

"Lexy?" He pointed over her shoulder. "That way."

"I know." She stopped directly in front of him, her smile broadening, and threw her arms around his neck. "Thank you, Matthew."

He stumbled back under her enthusiasm and his arms immediately came up to circle her waist. His right hand landed low on her back, his fingers molded to the curve of her buttocks.

She tilted her head back to bestow a smile on him. "Tasha and I will be as quiet as two little mice. You will see." Her eyes lit up. "And I will cook for you every night. And wash your clothes. I will pay you back, Matthew, for everything."

Stunned into silence, Matt stared into her earnest, upturned face. Her soft, rounded breasts were crushed against his chest, and her feminine scent was making him light-headed. Reflexively he tightened his hold, and his palms itched from the softness beneath them. If he moved his hand a mere inch he could cup her to him, force her to feel the sudden hardness straining his fly.

The thought shocked him, horrified him. He gulped in some air and released her. This time he would help Lexy with no strings attached.

Even if it killed him.

Chapter Eight

Lexy glanced in her bathroom mirror and smoothed her hair. She wondered what her parents would say about her haircut. None of the Constantine women from as far back as she could remember had ever kept their hair shorter than waist length.

Although she suspected they might have more to say about the dark circles under her eyes. She hadn't had but an hour of sleep last night. From the moment she and Matthew had agreed that she should move into his home, the evening had been a whirlwind of packing, transporting clothes and toys and trying to make sure they had their stories straight.

Poor Tasha seemed confused and that made Lexy feel horrible. The guilt for having to involve her daughter in this scheme ranked only a shade ahead of almost having kissed Matthew.

Lexy shuddered. It had been a mistake, a very dreadful mistake. She'd had no business initiating physical contact with him no matter how innocent. She knew how he affected her, how time had changed nothing in the attraction department. She would have to be more careful.

But of course, she might have nothing to worry

about. After he discovered the one small detail about her parents she'd neglected to mention, he might be sending her back to her apartment, anyway. She felt pretty rotten over the small omission, but she rationalized that, since her newfound information had come via Mrs. Hershey, it didn't count. How could Lexy have anything to report until she had firsthand knowledge?

Glancing at the clock, she took a deep breath. She was excited...nervous...exhausted. Not a good way to start their visit.

"Tasha," she called. "We have to hurry. The bus will be at the corner in ten minutes."

A second later, a dark head appeared in the doorway. Today Tasha had thankfully kept the hair adornment down to a minimum. Only two bows tied back her sable hair, one yellow and one pink.

Lexy smiled at her daughter and held out her hand. "Ready?"

Tasha's head bobbed up and down. "When are we going to that man's house again?"

Lexy sighed and crouched down to rub off some toothpaste lurking at the corner of Tasha's mouth. "Honey, please don't call him that man. What did I ask—?"

"I know, Mommy." Tasha grinned. "Popo."

Lexy let out a pent-up breath. If she couldn't keep Tasha and Matthew apart, the plan would be doomed. She forced a smile, took her daughter's hand again and told herself they could do this, over and over again, as they raced for the bus stop.

Mrs. Hershey had directed Lexy's parents to a motel on the other side of town, hoping that putting some distance between them and Lexy's apartment would help Lexy out. As soon as she and Tasha got off the bus, she realized that the motel was located halfway to Matthew's house.

Although, she wasn't sure how that mattered in the overall scheme of things. She and Matthew had planned on sticking to the renovation story. In doing so, they hoped a visit to Matthew's would be unnecessary.

Lexy checked the note she'd written to herself and headed toward the room number her brother had given her when she'd called them earlier. Before she could knock, the door flew open.

"Alessandra!" Her brother picked her up and twirled her around until she was dizzy. Laughing, she punched his arm until he put her down.

"Serge," she said, her head tilting way back. "You have grown."

He thumped his chest. "I am bigger than Papa now, and all our cousins."

At the mention of their cousins, the sudden threat of tears burned her eyes. Impatient, she blinked them away. She'd been so concerned with her devious plan, she'd forgotten how truly long it had been since she'd seen everyone, and how much she missed them all.

"You are so handsome, too," she said, reaching up to touch his familiar face.

"I know." He grinned, and she laughed. He might be bigger than an oak tree now, but he hadn't changed.

"Alessandra!"

Lexy recognized her sister's voice before she turned to see Danica's long, flowing chestnut hair. Lexy put a hand at the wild flutter in her chest. Her little sister had grown into such a beauty.

Lexy opened her arms and Dani flew from the adjoining room, enfolded Lexy in a big hug and nearly lifted her off the ground. Little Danica was now taller than Lexy.

Laughter bubbled to Lexy's throat as she grabbed hold of the door frame for support. "What is Mama feeding you two?" Lexy asked automatically in Hungarian.

Dani's hazel eyes twinkled. "I know English now."

With a mixture of pride and concern, Lexy said, "But you were studying German."

"Papa says I can only come to America if I learn English, so..." She waved an animated hand through the air in a gesture Lexy remembered well. "I learn English. It was a snip."

Serge sighed with disgust. "*Snap*. It was a snap."

Danica spun toward him and rattled off in Hungarian what she thought of his interruption, making Lexy laugh. Some things hadn't changed. Dani's famous temper was still intact.

Feeling a tug on her slacks, Lexy turned to find Tasha's wide eyes on her. As soon as she knew she had Lexy's attention, Tasha scooted back toward the small, semi-hidden alcove to the left of the door.

Guilt slivered down Lexy's spine. "Oh, honey, I'm sorry." She tried to coax her daughter toward her but she wouldn't budge.

"Can we go home now, Mommy?" Tasha whispered.

Smiling, Lexy dropped to a crouched position. Tasha was often shy around strangers. Her family could be overwhelming at times. "Don't you want to meet your aunt and uncle?"

Tasha pressed her tiny lips together and gave her head a firm shake.

"But they came such a long way to see you."

"I want to go home now." She folded her arms across her narrow chest in familiar defiance.

"Who is this?" Danica poked her head out the door and gave Tasha a dazzling smile.

Her lips pursing into a pout, Tasha stared down at her pink tennis shoes.

Lexy held up a hand when Danica started to approach them. A short distance away, another door opened and someone shrieked. Lexy would recognize her mother's scream anywhere. Behind the scream was a loud bellow.

She gave Tasha a quick hug. "I'm right here, okay, honey? I'm just going to say hello to Mama and Papa."

In the next instant, Lexy was being hugged and swirled and kissed until she wasn't sure if her feet were still touching the ground. Her father was a few pounds heavier, his voice a little raspier, his hair nearly all gray, but he looked terrific.

But no one looked as great as her mother. At fifty, Grazyna Constantine's complexion was still flawless. And, undoubtably with the assistance of the local drugstore, her hair was still blond.

Lexy smiled fondly through tear-filled eyes at her family and turned to introduce her daughter.

She blinked, her heart plummeting to her stomach. Tasha was gone.

MATT CHUGGED A fourth cup of coffee, foolishly hoping the extra caffeine would jolt some sanity into him. He was plenty awake, considering he'd had only two hours' sleep last night, and his adrenaline was going through the roof. But he was edgy, ill-tempered and lacking concentration.

His thoughts kept straying to Lexy and the promise that he'd made her, that everything would work out.

Right. Everything was going down the toilet. He was unprepared for his case this morning and he hadn't yet talked with Amanda.

He stared at the open file spread across his desk. He was overreacting. In truth, he'd actually been prepared for Margaret Howell's divorce filing against her husband for more than a week now, and within the next three hours, he intended to take the guy to the cleaners on behalf of his client. But something was bothering him about the case. He made an angry dash across the folder jacket with his pen. Something he couldn't pinpoint.

His secretary buzzed him to announce that Mrs. Howell had arrived at the same time Brad barged into Matt's office without knocking.

"Ready, killer?" Brad crossed the room and helped himself to the untouched cinnamon raisin bagel sitting on Matt's desk.

"What's up?"

Brad shrugged. "I thought I'd sit in under the guise of playing backup while I learn from the master."

Matt started gathering his papers. "Funny."

"I'm not joking. You have the best win record in this firm."

Matt eyed his friend. Brad was often arrogant, definitely laid-back, but never humble. Matt shrugged. But people changed. Lexy sure had. "Suit yourself. I'm meeting with Mrs. Howell first. Her husband and his pet shark won't get here for another hour."

Brad chuckled and checked his Rolex. "The large

conference room?'' he asked, and when Matt nodded, Brad gave him a two-finger salute and left with the half-eaten bagel.

A moment later, Matt had Mrs. Howell shown into his office. Behind her dark glasses, he expected her faded green eyes were red-rimmed. No matter how adamant most of his female clients were about a self-initiated divorce, he'd learned from experience to have a supply of tissues handy in his office.

He stood and extended his hand. Hers was cold and clammy. She sat immediately, and he could see that she was a little shaky.

''Would you like some coffee, Mrs. Howell?''

She sniffed and shook her head. ''He called last night. He wanted me to postpone the proceedings.''

Matt said nothing. He knew she was talking about her soon-to-be ex-husband. This last-ditch effort was a common ploy, especially with longtime marriages. If he had to, he'd point that out, but most women just needed to talk for a few minutes. They'd express their misgivings in weepy snatches, until their memory returned to the reasons they were divorcing the bastard in the first place.

If by some slim chance they didn't get that far, a little reminder from Matt was normally all they needed. He was happy to provide that service. Not just because a final settlement netted his firm a nice fee, but because he understood the dismal odds of a successful marriage.

Mrs. Howell reached for a tissue. ''He promised he wouldn't work so hard. He said he'll start coming home by five every day and that we'd take a vacation this year.''

He nodded and surreptitiously glanced at his watch.

"That's a big sacrifice for Marvin to make. He owns his own business."

"Not *his* business," Matt reminded the older woman. "You're entitled to half."

She sighed. "This isn't about money, Mr. Monroe."

"Of course not," he replied in his most soothing voice. "But we here at Wharton and Billingsley want to ensure you're well taken care of after the divorce."

At his last word, she openly sobbed. Quickly she adjusted her sunglasses, patted her puffy, sixties blond hairdo and composed herself. "And what about ten years from now? Will you make sure I have companionship?"

Matt paused for several respectful moments. "And if you take him back, are you certain he'll be there in ten years? Or even five?"

Her shoulders rose with a deep, inaudible breath. "He says he still loves me and I believe him."

Stalling, Matt picked up his pen. What the hell was he supposed to say to that? Finally, he said, "You didn't believe him last week or two months ago."

Her smile was sad. "Wrong choice of words. More than believe him, I trust him. He never lied to me. He'd made no secret that his business came first. I got tired of it. I told him no more playing second fiddle for me. Now he says I'm right, and he wants to make our marriage his priority."

He threw down the pen and leaned back in his chair while rolling his shoulders. He was tired, edgy and in serious need of a kick in the butt for not nipping this conversation in the bud. "Is this about your kids?"

"No." Her laugh was brief, dismissive. "Two are married and the last one is in college. This is about love, Mr. Monroe, and a long history together." She removed her sunglasses and blinked, suddenly looking lost, unsure. "Am I being a fool, Mr. Monroe? Am I allowing sentiment to delay the inevitable?"

Matt let out a long, slow, frustrated breath and an earthy word sprung to mind. He wasn't a friggin' guidance counselor. He met Mrs. Howell's anxious eyes, and something shifted inside him. When had he become so cynical? Maybe the man's priorities *had* changed. "You're not a fool. Go ahead and wait. Don't do anything more right now." He shrugged. "Let him move back in if you want. See what happens."

Mrs. Howell's lips started to curve, and although she looked nothing like her, damn if he didn't see Lexy's smile.

He pushed away from his desk, suddenly impatient with himself. This had nothing to do with Lexy. This was about how he'd just screwed his firm out of a hefty fee. Damn.

Mrs. Howell stood, her mouth stretched in a wide smile. "They were wrong about you, Mr. Monroe. I'm glad."

"It's too late to call your husband's attorney," he said, not wanting to know who *they* were or what they'd said. He was feeling foolish enough. "He's supposed to be here with your husband in twenty minutes."

"That's okay. I think I'll wait for them out in the lobby, if that's okay with you."

He opened the door and gestured expansively. "Of course. I'll have to speak to his attorney, naturally, but other than that, we're done."

She stood outside his office, still smiling. "Thank you again, Mr. Monroe. You're a very nice man."

Out of his peripheral vision, Matt saw his secretary's head come up. Behind her, Brad folded his arms across his chest. What? They didn't think he was a nice guy?

"You take care and call when you decide what you want to do." He watched her head for the overstuffed sofas near the elevators.

Now that his afternoon was suddenly clear, it would be smart to get ahold of Amanda. He'd hate for her to show up at his house and find Lexy's clothes all over the place. And the way his day was going...

"What happened?" Brad asked in a low voice, his gaze sweeping toward Mrs. Howell's retreating back.

"She changed her mind."

"So? Most of them do at some point."

Just as Matt turned to go back into his office, he thought he heard Amanda's voice. He stopped, squinting at her father's closed door. "Is Amanda in there?"

Brad gaped at him. "This is the first client you let slip through your fingers and you're acting like it's no big deal. Are you nuts?"

He lifted a brow. "The woman has a right to change her mind. Divorce is slightly more important than deciding what's for dinner tonight." He abruptly turned to his secretary and caught her exchanging a stunned look with Brad. He felt his patience slip. They were acting like he was some kind of monster. "Is Amanda in her father's office, or not?"

The secretary nodded, picked up a stack of papers and headed for the copy room.

"I'm glad you're biting everyone's head off this morning and not just mine," Brad said. "No wonder Mrs. Howell couldn't wait to get out of here."

"Since you obviously have nothing to do, tell

Amanda to stop by my office when she comes out."
Matt was about to close his door when Brad pushed
his way in behind him.

"If you think I'm hanging around when old man
Wharton hears about how you screwed up this account, you're in worse shape than I thought. It won't
matter squat that you're marrying his daughter."

Matt rammed a weary hand through his hair. "For
heaven's sake, the woman still loves her husband.
What was I supposed to do?"

"Let them reconcile later. After the legal proceedings. Ring any bells?" Brad pulled back the chair. "I
believe those were your famous last—"

"Don't get comfortable," Matt said before his
friend could sit.

Someone knocked at the door. Brad shook his head
and lowered his voice. "You think the old man found
out already?"

"Goodbye, Brad."

The door opened and Amanda ducked her head inside. When she saw that only Brad was with him, she
advanced. "I don't suppose you're free for lunch."

"He is now," Brad said, sending Matt a sympa-
thetic glance as he let himself out.

A slight frown puckered her perfectly shaped eyebrows. She didn't always care for Brad. He was often
too earthy for her tastes. "What was that about?"

"Nothing. He's just…" Matt waved a dismissive
hand. He didn't want to get into it with her. Not that
they often discussed his cases, or the firm, or anything
else for that matter. He pursed his lips, suddenly curious about her reaction. "It's about this case I've been
working on. The woman changed her mind, said she
wanted to think about taking her husband back."

"Does that mean you lose your fee?"

"Not all of it."

Her blue eyes narrowed. "But most of it, right?"

He nodded.

"You don't look upset."

He sank into his chair, chuckling. "Yeah, I guess I'm not."

"You've totally lost me, Matt."

"Love, Amanda," he said, studying her bewildered expression with mixed emotions. She didn't understand. For whatever unfathomable reason, he wanted her to, but he hadn't really expected it. "True love won out."

She stared at him for a long, silent moment. "I hope you get some rest before the wedding. You haven't been yourself lately."

The funny thing was, she didn't look worried or curious, merely put out. Even stranger, Matt felt indifferent to her obvious lack of concern.

He smiled. "Your hair is lighter, isn't it?"

She laughed and touched a blond tendril that had slipped from her usual French twist. "No." Then she glanced at her watch. He'd given it to her for her last birthday. She'd been disappointed it wasn't a diamond bracelet. Of course, she hadn't *said* a word. If nothing else, Amanda had been raised with class. But he saw the disappointment in her eyes whenever she checked the time. "I have to drop the invitations off at the post office," she said, "but I could swing back by here for lunch."

"Good. I need to talk to you."

"Anything important?"

He half smiled. "Not really."

She stopped at the door. "Is Daddy going to be in a bad mood this afternoon?"

"Probably."

"Hmmm. Maybe I won't tell him I decided on white orchids for the reception until tomorrow. I'm already over budget."

The phone rang, and angling his head to see if his secretary had returned, Matt saw her pick up the receiver. He looked back at Amanda. "Any place in particular for lunch?"

"How does French sound?"

"I'll ask Carol to make reservations. One o'clock all right?"

"Mr. Monroe?" Carol popped her head in the door. "There's a call for you."

He frowned at his secretary's uncharacteristic interruption. "Can't you take a message?"

"I don't think so." Her gaze darted to Amanda. "Her name is Lexy Monroe and she says it's urgent."

Chapter Nine

"Lexy?" Matthew paused at the open door.

Sitting alone in the quiet motel room, she looked up, her tear-stained face flushed and blotchy. "Matthew!" She gave him a watery smile. "You're here."

He opened his arms to her. "Honey, we'll find Tasha."

The bed creaked as she stood, and dabbing at her face, she came to him. He put his arms around her and hugged her close. Her body was rigid with tension, and her heart beat frantically against his chest.

"You're going to be mad," she said, starting to pull back.

He wouldn't let her distance herself. Keeping her snug against him, he stroked her back. "Of course I won't be mad," he said soothingly. She wasn't making sense. Clearly she was too upset. "Just calm down and tell me exactly what happened. We'll find her. I promise."

She sniffed. "We already have."

"What?" His hands froze in the middle of her back.

A rustling noise came from behind a closed door, presumably the bathroom. From outside, a boisterous round of rapid and foreign conversation grew louder as the speakers approached.

"You found her?" he asked, torn between relief and irritation.

Lexy tilted her head back and nodded. Her eyes were still red from crying. The dark circles were probably from lack of sleep. "She was at a pay phone trying to call Mrs. Hershey. She's in the bathroom right now."

"Well, good."

She winced. "Except, now my parents know you're in town when we'd planned to tell them you'd be gone for a week. I'm sorry, Matthew, I shouldn't have called you. I just—"

He ran his palm down her back. "That's okay. You did the right thing." Mentally, he cursed. What were they going to do now? "Does she normally run off like this?"

Lexy sighed and stepped back. "No, but she felt a little overwhelmed with my family." She bit her lower lip. "Whom you are about to meet at any second."

The voices outside grew menacingly loud and then there was utter silence. Matthew didn't have to turn around to know they all stood in the doorway.

Right now, he'd almost rather be in old Judge "Hardnose" Harding's courtroom. And that said a lot.

He winked at Lexy. "A kiss for luck?"

Her eyes rounded.

He swooped down before she could react further and kissed her surprised mouth. The kiss was brief, nonthreatening, but when their eyes met, he knew it had been a mistake. The instant longing he found in her gaze matched his own, and for the first time, he admitted to himself he was looking forward to this charade.

She gave him a weak smile, then moved to the side and signaled to her family.

Slowly Matthew turned around.

Two men pinned him with intense stares. They were huge, several inches taller than himself, and probably outweighed him by forty pounds each. The graying older man wore that same strange red vest over his barrel-like chest. Although he was on the paunchy side, Matt's money would be on him in a barroom brawl.

The younger one had wavy black hair and reminded Matt of that Jethro character on the old *Beverly Hill-billies* show. Except, women usually went for this type of guy. Matt hoped he had more brawn than brains. He assumed this was the brother, the one family member who knew English.

Lexy cleared her throat. She said a few words in Hungarian to them. He only recognized his name. Then she turned to him and said, "Matthew, this is my father, Boris Constantine, and my brother, Serge."

Matt stuck out his hand and hoped these guys wouldn't rather head-butt.

Boris Constantine was the first to step forward. His swarthy, bearded face split into a wide grin and he pumped Matt's hand with enthusiasm. "It is my honor, Matthew Monroe. My daughter tells me much good about you."

English. The guy had just spoken English. Broken English, heavily accented English, but still English...

What was going on?

Matt slid Lexy a murderous look.

She winced and gave him a small, helpless shrug.

Boris stepped back, and before Matt could flex his crushed hand, Serge nearly yanked Matt's arm off.

"I am Serge. You are good to my sister, yes?"

Yeah, right. Like Matt had a choice here. He smiled wryly at the younger man. "You bet."

Serge frowned, then grinned and turned to his father. "That means yes."

"Mama, Danica, come." Lexy plowed through the two men, who promptly stepped aside.

She reached out a hand and a beautiful blond woman stepped forward. She was about fifty or so, and made a great case for the May-September romance proponents.

Her eyes met Matt's, their vivid blue shade startling him. *The exact same color as Natasha's.* He blinked at the sharp stab of disappointment that made his heart trip.

This was good, right? Didn't this erase any doubts? He should be overjoyed.

But he suddenly felt out of sorts and vaguely uneasy, as though he'd been tossed in the middle of the Ohio River in a rowboat with no oars. It was an odd, annoying feeling, especially when his next thought jumped to Tasha's mysterious father—the man with whom Lexy had chosen to bear a child.

He hadn't realized he'd extended his hand again until it got crushed between him and Lexy's mother. She grabbed him in a huge hug, her strong, flowery scent nearly smothering him.

Matt glanced helplessly at Lexy. His thoughts had gone so haywire, he hadn't even caught her mother's name.

Laughing, Lexy said something to her mother in Hungarian, and the woman finally backed off. But as she pulled away, she kept Matt's hands in her firm grip and looked at him with tears in her eyes.

"You make my Alessandra very happy," she said.

Oh, great. They all speak English. He forced himself not to look at Lexy. He had plenty of time to strangle her later. "I try," he assured her mother with a strained smile.

"Grazyna is very hard for Americans," she said slowly. "You call me Grace."

She spoke with such labored concentration, her accent as thick as his grandmother's brown gravy, that renewed hope swelled within him. Maybe they only knew a few practiced phrases.

Next she turned up his palm, her eyebrows lifting as she studied it, and she murmured something he couldn't understand.

Lexy quickly tugged his hand free from her mother's grasp. "And this is my sister, Danica," Lexy said, transferring his hand to a much smaller one. "But she likes to be called Dani."

Like Lexy, her sister was on the petite side, about five-five if he were to guess, maybe a little taller. And she was pretty, too. Though not half as attractive as Lexy.

She beamed up at him, her bright hazel eyes twinkling with curiosity as she made no secret of sizing him up. After giving him a quick hug, she went back to looking him over.

"You are not what I accept, Matthew," she finally said.

No one said anything, least of all Matt. Her bluntness took him by surprise.

Lexy made a small, helpless sound of exasperation, while the elder Constantines looked confused.

Serge sighed with pure disgust. "*Expected*, Dani. He is not what you *expected*." He waved an expansive hand through the air, shaking his head in big-brother irritation. "How many times I tell you, you must study your English harder. But no, you have a date with this one and that one, and all of them no good."

Dani's hands flew to her hips, her eyes narrowing, and she advanced on her brother, her stalking rhythm reminding Matt of a wildcat about to tear apart her enemy.

Boris stepped between them, and with one bellow, everyone froze.

Matt didn't understand the Hungarian word, but he could read the menacing expression on the older man's face. He'd seen it enough when his father had to break up fights between Matt and his brothers. The unexpected memory gave him an even more unexpected pang of longing. It had been too long since he'd seen his family.

Dani flipped back her long, shiny hair and gave Matt a sheepish look, a kind of fleeting apology before her megawatt smile returned.

One side of Matt's mouth curved, too. "You all aren't exactly what I expected, either."

Lexy cleared her throat. "I'd better check on Tasha."

He threw her a don't-you-dare-leave-me look, but it was too late. She knocked briefly on the bathroom door, then opened it and stepped inside.

Matt turned back to Boris Constantine's unreadable expression. "Well..." Matt rubbed his hands together, his gaze wandering over to Serge, who stared back with a goofy grin plastered across his face. "How about them White Sox?"

Two pairs of dark eyebrows dipped in confusion.

"Matthew? Would you come here, please?" Lexy called.

"You got it." He gestured toward the bathroom, hoping they understood why he was about to make tracks. But he didn't wait for a response. As it was he couldn't get his feet to move fast enough.

The moment he saw the little girl huddled in the corner, hunched down between the sink and the wall, he forgot about everyone else. She looked so small and fragile and scared as hell.

His stomach constricting, his gaze found Lexy's anxious one. "Is she sick?"

At the sound of his voice, Tasha looked up. Her eyes widened and lit up like a string of Christmas lights, and she gave him a shy smile.

Speechless, he leaned on the door frame. Nothing prepared him for the sheer joy her reception gave him. His heart skipped two beats, then somersaulted like it had the first day of the circus when he was five.

"Hi, Tasha," he said. "Are you playing hide-and-seek?"

She shook her head. "I want to go home," she whispered.

He could barely hear her, so he lowered himself to a crouched position. Mistaking his intentions, Tasha scrambled up, then scooted over to him.

She put a hand on his shoulder. "Will you take Mommy and me home?"

Matt stared into her pleading blue eyes, and suddenly he resented the hell out of Tasha's grandmother. He slowly lifted a hand to brush a stubborn tear off her cheek with his thumb. Never had he touched skin so soft, so vulnerable, and Matt felt more humbled than he thought he was capable of feeling.

"That depends on Mommy, honey." He glanced at Lexy. She was faintly shaking her head, her dazed expression a blend of surprise…panic.

"Mommy?" Tasha tugged on her hand.

Lexy blinked, then she crouched down, too. Tasha put her free hand on Lexy's knee. Her other one she kept on his shoulder. "Tasha. Your grandpa and grandma came a long way to meet you. Can you talk to them for a little while? I know Grandpa has a big voice, but he doesn't mean to scare you."

The little girl frowned, her lower lip beginning to jut.

Matt let a slow smile curve his lips. "Is that what's the matter? Is your grandpa scaring you?"

Wordlessly, she stared down at her tennis shoes.

"What about if you were bigger than him?" Matt asked. "Would that make you feel better?"

Curiosity won and she raised her chin by several halting degrees to look at him. "How?"

"Well, let's see." Matt rubbed his jaw. "If you ate all your vegetables…"

She tilted her head to the side and gave him a skeptical look, clearly unimpressed with his teasing.

He grinned. "Or you can sit on my shoulders. That way you can see the top of his head."

Her gaze widened and flicked to her mother. Lexy was smiling a smile that made it all the way up to her beautiful, glistening brown eyes. And Matt's heart beat a little faster.

Tasha leaned against him, and in a small, shy voice she said, "Okay."

WELCOME TO THE
CASINO!

Try your luck at the Roulette Wheel ...
Play a hand of Twenty-One!

How to play:

1. Play the Roulette and Twenty-One scratch-off games, as instructed on the opposite page, to see that you are eligible for FREE BOOKS and a FREE GIFT!

2. Send back the card and you'll receive TWO brand-new Harlequin American Romance® novels. These books have a cover price of $3.99 each in the U.S. and $4.50 each in Canada, but they are yours to keep absolutely free.

3. There's no catch. You're under no obligation to buy anything. We charge nothing — ZERO — for your first shipment. And you don't have to make any minimum number of purchases — not even one!

4. The fact is, thousands of readers enjoy receiving books by mail from the Harlequin Reader Service® before they're available in stores. They like the convenience of home delivery, and they love our discount prices!

5. We hope that after receiving your free books you'll want to remain a subscriber. But the choice is yours — to continue or cancel, any time at all!
So why not take us up on our invitation, with no risk of any kind. You'll be glad you did!

Play Twenty-One For This Exquisite Free Gift!

THIS SURPRISE
MYSTERY GIFT
WILL BE YOURS
FREE WHEN YOU PLAY
TWENTY-ONE

It's fun, and we're giving away *FREE GIFTS* to all players!

PLAY ROULETTE!

Scratch the silver to see that the ball has landed on 7 RED, making you eligible for TWO FREE romance novels!

PLAY TWENTY-ONE!

Scratch the silver to reveal a winning hand! Congratulations, you have Twenty-One. Return this card promptly and you'll receive a fabulous free mystery gift, along with your free books!

YES!

Please send me all the free Harlequin American Romance® books and the gift for which I qualify! I understand that I am under no obligation to purchase any books, as explained on the back of this card.

Name: _____
(PLEASE PRINT)

Address: _____ Apt.#: _____

City: _____ State: _____ Zip: _____

Offer limited to one per household and not valid to current Harlequin American Romance® subscribers. All orders subject to approval.   PRINTED IN U.S.A.

354 HDL CQX6   **154 HDL CQXQ**
                                    (H-AR-09/99)

The Harlequin Reader Service® — Here's how it works:

Accepting your 2 free books and mystery gift places you under no obligation to buy anything. You may keep the books and gift and return the shipping statement marked "cancel." If you do not cancel, about a month later we'll send you 4 additional novels and bill you just $3.34 each in the U.S., or $3.71 each in Canada, plus 25¢ delivery per book and applicable taxes if any.* That's the complete price and — compared to the cover price of $3.99 in the U.S. and $4.50 in Canada — it's quite a bargain! You may cancel at any time, but if you choose to continue, every month we'll send you 4 more books, which you may either purchase at the discount price or return to us and cancel your subscription.

*Terms and prices subject to change without notice. Sales tax applicable in N.Y. Canadian residents will be charged applicable provincial taxes and GST.

"Good." He braced himself against the wall, preparing to accept her slight weight. "Ready?"

"Uh-huh."

Lexy stood and turned Tasha so that her back faced Matt. Then she slipped her hands under her daughter's arms.

Matt anchored his hands around her tiny waist. "On the count of three," he said.

"One," Lexy said, and the delighted laughter in her voice made his heart expand.

"Two," Tasha added, breathless.

"Three," Matt and Lexy said together, and hoisted her up at the same time.

Tasha settled on his shoulders, gasping as she searched for a hold and finding one by hugging his head, her palms ending up across his eyes.

"Hey, pumpkin, how am I supposed to see?" Matt urged her hands to his neck, and giggling, Tasha complied. "Ready for me to stand up? You have to watch your head when we go through the door."

"I'm ready," she said softly.

Slowly he rose to a standing position, vaguely wondering if all little girls had this pleasant powdery smell. Then making sure Tasha was well balanced, he turned them around to rejoin Lexy's family and met with four pairs of approving eyes.

A sense of deep contentment filled him. Or maybe relief was more accurate. He and Lexy had been worried for nothing. If they weren't the picture of the perfect little happy family right now, he didn't know what was.

Pleased that they'd just made it over the first and possibly worst hurdle, he glanced over at Lexy.

Taken aback, he frowned.

Why was she crying?

LEXY COULD hardly force down another bite of her tuna salad sandwich. Her throat was too clogged with emotion. So much had happened in just a couple of hours, what with seeing her family after such a long separation, Tasha disappearing, and then having to see Matthew and Tasha together. The way the two of them seemed to have bonded had probably been the biggest blow of all. She hadn't expected Tasha to take to Matthew so well. And Lexy certainly hadn't been prepared for the tender way Matthew had responded. Had she been wrong in keeping the truth from him? From Tasha? The possibility turned her stomach.

Dealing with her parents ran a close second as far as problems went. It astonished her that after eight years away from them, she could still feel like she was ten years old again. But she did. All it took was one disapproving or quizzical look from her father.

"Why are you not eating?" her mother asked in slow, halting English. "You are too thin."

Lexy smiled, knowing better than to argue. All eyes were on her and she took a conciliatory nibble. She started to say something in Hungarian but abandoned the effort. They wanted to practice English, they had reminded her several times, in order to include Tasha and Matthew in their conversations.

Well, Matthew had returned to his office immediately after getting Tasha to rejoin the family, declining almost too quickly to come across the street to the coffee shop with them. Lexy hadn't minded. She was still too attracted to him. And the gentle way he handled their daughter turned her to mush. Being around him was going to be more difficult than she'd thought.

"It's close to dinnertime," Lexy said slowly, and glanced at Tasha, who was still very quiet, also barely touching the sandwich they shared. Quiet wasn't a bad thing, considering the circumstances.

Sitting to her right, Serge nudged her with his elbow. With his eyes, he signaled his desire for her untouched potato chips.

Lexy laughed and pushed the plate toward him. He immediately dug in, ignoring their mother's disgusted sigh.

"He eats like this still," she said. "Like he is a young…" Frowning, clearly at a loss for the correct word, she let her voice trail off.

"Bull," Serge supplied between bites. "Horse."

Her mother nodded with a resigned look. Then she straightened and pointed to herself. "Tonight I will cook."

Lexy blinked. "Tonight?"

"You want *kofte* and *begendi?*"

Normally, talk of the lamb meatballs and the eggplant-and-cheese dish handed down from the Turkish side of her father's family would have made Lexy's mouth water. But right now, panic swelled her tongue and blocked her air passage.

She moistened her lips. "I think we should eat in a restaurant tonight."

Her brother and father both frowned.

Dani quickly agreed. "And we dance after?"

"No." Serge held up a finger. "You are here to visit Alessandra."

"You are not the king, Serge," Dani shot back.

"Enough," their father said in Hungarian, his

abrupt order silencing everyone. "We will eat at Alessandra's house. We are her…"

"Guests," Serge said, finishing with a smirk aimed at Dani.

Lexy took a deep breath. She had prepared for this. She had a plan. Everything would be fine. Of course, the original idea was that she'd tell them Matthew was out of town, but now they knew better.

"We can go to my old apartment," she said brightly, "since Matthew will be working late. The kitchen is small but not too much smaller than the one at home. It is not as bad a place as it looks. It is very convenient to my job and Tasha's school. That's why Matthew let me keep it as I have already explained. We can stop at the grocery store and pick up what we need and—"

She cut herself off when her nervous chattering was met with four blank stares. Her voice was unnaturally high, and she'd spoken too quickly. She doubted even Serge had kept up with her. Even Tasha was gazing at her in wide-eyed amazement. She hoped her daughter didn't choose to finally open up and start asking tricky questions.

After taking a deep, steadying breath, she repeated everything in Hungarian. Before she was finished, her father started shaking his head, a sad and disapproving expression on his bearded face.

She didn't have to ask what he found objectionable about her suggestion. She'd seen the same look on his face earlier. In fact, disappointment had shown on all their faces at least once today.

Lexy understood the problem. It had been eating at her for the past two hours. They thought she was too American, that she'd forgotten their simple country ways, and that now family no longer came first. They couldn't understand why she had not invited them to stay in her house, to share each meal at her table. It mattered little that Lexy had explained her carefully practiced house-remodeling excuse. If the situation were reversed, no sacrifice would be too great to accommodate her and Tasha and Matthew. It was the Gypsy way.

But to them, she was an American now, with an American husband and daughter, and a comfortable American life. And they felt like second-class citizens with their own daughter. Ironically, they believed she didn't care enough.

But they were wrong. She cared, all right. Maybe too much. That's why she was in this mess.

"Okay," she said, her common sense crumpling like a used paper napkin. "Dinner will be at our house."

Chapter Ten

Matt put Amanda's pink roses in some water, then started tearing open the packages of food he'd picked up from the Maisonnette on the way home. The restaurant's chef had taken pity on him and prepared two of Amanda's favorite dishes at the last minute. For extra measure, Matt had also picked up an expensive bottle of cabernet. He suspected he was in quite a bit of trouble with her by now.

First he'd run out of his office with a vague excuse, then he'd stood her up for lunch. Later in the afternoon, he'd been too busy getting chewed out by her irate father to return her phone call. Fortunately he'd caught her an hour ago as she was headed out shopping. They only spoke for a minute...just long enough for him to grovel and invite her to dinner. And Matt was not a groveler.

After heating the oven to the exact temperature the chef had coached him on, he deposited the containers of lamb and veal and poached asparagus and baby red potatoes. Then he picked up his discarded suit jacket from the bar stool and started to unroll his shirtsleeves.

He had only a few minutes before she was to arrive and he wanted to make sure everything was perfect.

If he didn't soften her up before he dropped the bomb, no telling how she'd react. Amanda was a little high-strung at times. Usually he ignored her outbursts and they disappeared relatively quickly. But timing was important tonight. By tomorrow, Lexy's parents could be descending upon their pseudo home. He'd had no time to talk to Lexy today about the new plan. Whatever that was. He only knew the old one was in the toilet.

He still wasn't sure how much he wanted to tell Amanda…other than as little as possible.

The doorbell rang. He checked his watch and backed up toward the door while giving the dining room table a final inspection. Her favorite pink roses were in the center, the red cabernet was opened and breathing….

Everything looked good.

He started to open the door, noticed his suit jacket still lying across his arm and ditched it in the coat closet. The doorbell sounded again—one short impatient buzz. While finger-combing his hair with one hand, he opened the door with the other.

She stood with her arms folded across her chest, her left foot tapping. Not a good sign. "I thought you stood me up again," Amanda said, and waited a pointed five seconds before walking past him into the house.

Clearly she hadn't forgiven him. This was going to be a long night. He closed the door, using the momentary distraction to plaster a smile across his face, when what he really wanted to do was cut loose with a word that would shock her. He was tired and grouchy himself, and in no mood to put up with any attitude. But he'd already ticked off her father, and

Matt figured one Wharton grabbing him by the short hairs was enough for one day.

Amanda turned and surprised him with a pleasant smile. "I see you've been working hard. The flowers are a nice touch. What's in the oven, veal or lamb?"

"Both. Raspberry torte for later."

Her smile widened.

He was home free. Which both pleased and irritated him. Why *did* he have to work so hard for Amanda's understanding? Actually, her sudden change in attitude had little to do with understanding. In her eyes, he needed forgiveness…magnanimous forgiveness.

Lexy wouldn't have whined or arched her brows in silent disapproval when he'd begged off earlier and said he had to help a friend, no matter how vague or brief his explanation. She would have respected his loyalty.

Mentally he shook his head. He had no business comparing Amanda to Lexy. No business at all. "I'll pour you some wine," he said. "Or would you prefer a martini first and save the wine for dinner?"

She bowed her head over the roses and sniffed, her blue silk dress perfectly cut for her slender form. Her legs were long and shapely, her hair angelic blond. By most men's standards, she was a knockout. She was also well bred, well educated and she made a terrific hostess.

He ought to consider himself lucky.

And he did.

In spite of her temper…her selfish bends…the way she ran to Daddy for everything…

"Did you hear me?" she asked, frowning. "Where has your mind suddenly wandered? You look like the hounds of hell are after you."

He inhaled deeply, smiled. "Sorry."

"I said, I'll have a martini, but only if you have cocktail onions…oh, and dry vermouth."

"Of course."

She called out another request before he made it through the kitchen door, but he didn't hear all of it and decided not to stop and ask. He had a feeling he was in for a lifetime of special requests. Why get a head start?

Quickly he mixed their drinks, and felt only slightly guilty for making Amanda's with an extra kick. The mellower she was, the better. Second thoughts over Lexy's plan were making him crazy enough. So far, everything that could go wrong had done just that. Her parents spoke English, and they knew he was in town.

The more he'd rehearsed his speech to Amanda on the way home, the more hopeless the plan's success sounded. Depending on how his fiancée reacted to his fabricated accounting of his unavailability for the next two weeks, he was seriously thinking about telling Lexy he had to bow out.

Not that he would outright abandon her, but if necessary, they could tell her parents he was leaving town for the rest of their stay. Then he'd put Lexy and Tasha up in some nice apartment at his expense.

He carried their drinks into the living room and found Amanda settled into one of the wing chairs. He handed a martini to her—the one with the cocktail onions and extra zing.

"We have an extremely busy couple of weeks ahead," she said, and he groaned to himself.

He took a long, cool sip and a seat on the sofa. "What's on the agenda?" he asked slowly.

"Wedding decisions mostly."

He nodded, feeling somewhat relieved. "Then you don't need me."

She cocked her head to the side and studied him for an uncomfortable minute. "Getting cold feet?"

"Why would you say that?" he asked, taken aback not only by the question but by her dispassionate tone.

She sipped and shrugged. "Maybe it's just me. I've been a little stressed."

Great. Now he felt guilty for bailing out on her. Yet, Amanda had made it clear from the beginning that his input was not only unnecessary but unwelcome. He'd tried not to take it personally. She was blue-blood, he was blue-collar. He could forget that fact, but sometimes, she couldn't. "How about you? Cold feet?"

She met his eyes directly. "Of course not. The invitations are already in the mail."

He stared back at her, uneasiness making his jaw tighten. Maybe he was experiencing some prewedding jitters. Except he felt more numb than anything. "Is there something you want me to do?"

She toyed with the stem of her glass, looking thoughtful. "Not really."

"Well, good…" He took a gulp. "I'm going to be pretty tied up for the next couple of weeks."

She wrinkled her nose. "Is Daddy keeping you that busy so close to the wedding?"

"No. It's personal." He paused, harboring the slim hope she'd leave it at that. But she lifted an expectant brow, and he added, "I'm helping out an old friend."

"Ah, yes, the friend. Anyone I know?"

The oven timer buzzed and, relieved, Matt jumped to his feet. "Dinner's ready," he mumbled.

"Want some help?"

Already halfway to the kitchen, he held up a hand.

"No, you just relax. In fact, pour yourself some wine."

He hurried through the door before she could say another word and quickly emptied the oven before he screwed up dinner by drying everything out. He could only locate one pot holder, so supplementing it with an apron, he carried two plates of steaming food into the dining room.

"Come have a seat," he called to her. "I'll get the asparagus and salads and be right with you."

"It smells divine," she said, leaving her chair and coming toward him.

At the same time the doorbell rang.

They exchanged frowns, and she asked, "Are you expecting anyone?" When he shook his head, she shrugged and offered to get it.

He slid the plates onto the table, wondering who could possibly be dropping in at this hour. And then a sudden, horrible thought occurred to him.

His pulse accelerated.

Nah, she wouldn't just show up unannounced like this....

He flung the pot holder onto the table. The apron strings tangled with his fingers and he cursed, taking the apron with him as he rushed to the door. "Amanda, wait..."

It was too late. She opened the door.

Lexy and her family stood outside. Lexy's tentative smile started to fade by several painful degrees as her gaze froze on Amanda, then slowly moved to Matt. Towering behind his daughter, Boris Constantine wore a stunned expression that turned into a scowl, his dark eyes bulging, his forehead creasing like a mad bulldog's.

Amanda's brows arched. "What do you—"

"Amanda." Matt stepped between her and the Constantines and shoved the apron at her. She was using that haughty tone he so despised, and with the murderous way Boris was looking, World War Three couldn't be far off. "There are two more dishes in the oven."

Stunned into silence, she gaped at him.

Seizing the opportunity, he placed his hands on her shoulders and turned her toward the kitchen. He was going to pay for this. Dearly.

She shook away from him and turned to glare first at him, and then at their unexpected guests. "Matthew, if you think that—"

He straightened, giving her his back and smiling at Boris, then he shrugged. "Good help is so hard to find."

Behind him, Amanda shrieked. In the next second, the apron slapped his back and slid to the floor.

Matt swore under his breath. He'd hoped she hadn't heard that remark. The ruse was clearly over. Amanda was never going to understand what had just happened. He was going to be trying to explain it from now until their tenth anniversary.

"What is going on in there?" Serge popped up behind Lexy and poked his head in the door. When his gaze rested on Amanda, his head jerked back in surprise. At least he looked too stunned to want to strangle Matt with his bare hands, unlike Boris, who continued to glare at Matt with open hostility.

Great. Just friggin' great.

Matt looked at Lexy. Obviously she needed to come clean. Except she looked pretty shocked herself, her face so sickly pale that it made him feel ill himself.

He started to go to her, then stopped and reluctantly glanced over his shoulder.

Fury blotched Amanda's face an undignified red. Her eyes were blazing hotter than during any temper tantrum he'd so far witnessed. Yet she was his fiancée, the woman he was to marry, and by all rights, the person who should command his loyalty. But then there was Lexy…frightened…panicked…vulnerable.

He wavered for another moment, feeling like the frayed rope in a game of tug-of-war. And then he stepped forward, took Lexy's hand and pulled her into his arms.

She stiffened for a second, then sagged against him.

At the sound of glass shattering behind him, he winced. Lexy pulled back, her eyes wide and liquid, and she whispered, "I'm sorry, Matthew. I told them I lost my house key. I tried—"

"Hey." He gave her a small one-shoulder shrug. "You'd better go talk to her."

He brushed a lone tear from her cheek. "Yeah."

Before he could go to Amanda, Serge pushed his way inside the house. He looked like a mad bull as his gaze scanned the rooms. As soon as he saw Amanda slamming through the kitchen door, he headed toward her with obvious purpose.

"Oh-oh." Lexy made a face.

Matt had the insane urge to grab Lexy and run, and let Serge handle Amanda. And then he came to his senses. "You take care of your parents," he told Lexy. "Take them to the living room."

"I'd better come with you." She turned to her family, and gesturing toward the living room, she delivered a rush of Hungarian. To Tasha, who'd just peeked her head in, Lexy said, "Stay with Grandma and Grandpa."

Matt didn't hang around to argue. He had already lit off for the kitchen door, through which Serge had just disappeared after Amanda. It was quiet in there. Too damn quiet.

Gingerly, he pushed the door open.

Serge's hands were around Amanda's waist, and she was sitting on the counter near the stove as though he'd just put her there. She swung back a hand holding a black cast-iron skillet in threat.

Sitting up high as she was, her glare evenly met Serge's. "Come on, you brute, make my day."

"I saw that movie," Serge said, thumping his chest with one hand. "Five times." His other hand remained fastened to Amanda's waist. "That Dirty Harry, he is not such a big man. I could squash him like this." For emphasis, Serge ground the heel of his hand on the counter near Amanda's leg.

Her dress had risen up to an indecent level, and Serge's finger brushed her nylon-encased thigh. Narrowing her incredulous eyes first on the offending hand and then on his face, she let out a low growl. "Do you know who I am?"

Serge ducked his head and met her narrowed gaze with a stern one of his own. "A pesky little ant." Then he straightened. "Too bad. You could be very pretty little woman."

Sheer amazement held Matt immobile as he watched the stunned disbelief flash across Amanda's outraged face. She was going to chew this guy up and spit him out at any minute, and God help Matt, but he wasn't sure he wanted to stop it.

Lexy pushed in behind him. "What's going on?"

Serge and Amanda both jerked their heads around, and spotting Lexy and Matt, they both started talking at once.

Matt sighed and walked farther into the kitchen. This couldn't be happening. "Amanda, please put down the skillet."

"You tell this…this…Neanderthal to get away from me," she said, raising her weapon.

Lexy said something in Hungarian, the foreign words curt, forceful.

Serge let out a long, exasperated sigh, and in a flash, relieved Amanda of the skillet. Circling her waist with his hands again, he lifted her off the counter and lowered her until her feet touched the floor.

She held her ground for a tense moment, staring up at Serge, her hands balling into fists.

As impossible as it seemed, Matt feared she was going to deck the guy, and he stepped forward, ready to intervene. But before he could do or say anything, Amanda uncurled her hands, smoothed down her dress, lifted her chin and in an amazingly calm voice said, "Kindly step aside."

One side of Serge's mouth hiked up in a slow, considering grin, then he gave her a short bow and did as she asked.

"Matthew," Amanda said, her distrusting eyes still trained on Serge. "I'd like to see you in your study."

"Uh, sure." Matt made eye contact with Lexy and signaled her to follow.

She shook her head, but as Amanda strolled by in her normal lady-of-the-manor fashion, he jerked Lexy's hand and whispered, "It'll look suspicious if Amanda and I disappear alone."

"I'll make an excuse for you."

"Lexy." He made her name a warning.

"Matthew?" With her palm pressed to the door, Amanda paused without turning around.

"Coming." He tightened his hold on Lexy's hand. "You don't have to say a word," he said, and pulled her along with him.

He didn't blame her for being afraid of Amanda. The woman could spit fire when she was so inclined. Matt and her father were the only ones she didn't push too hard. The fact that she hadn't handed Serge his head on a platter was one for the record books.

Matt chuckled softly just thinking about the scene in the kitchen as they followed Amanda through the living room, until Lexy's dirty look shut him up. She called out something in Hungarian to her family as they sat watching the parade, the two women staring wide-eyed, her father looking as though he were contemplating homicide.

"What did you just tell them?" Matt asked in a low voice as they entered his study.

Wincing, Lexy shot a look at Amanda's back, then hesitantly whispered, "That our maid was unhappy because they arrived early and we needed to talk to her."

Amanda stopped. Slowly she turned around, her face beginning to color, shock and irritation warring for dominance.

Matt urged Lexy into the room, forcing Amanda to back up, then quickly shut the door before Amanda blew. Not that a simple six-panel, three-inch-thick, solid oak door would contain what he knew she had to say.

"Matthew James Monroe..." Amanda began, her voice tight as she obviously struggled for control.

Matt held up a silencing hand before she could start in on him. "I was just about to explain this to you, Amanda. Remember I said I needed to help a friend out?" he asked, slanting Lexy a glance. Her eyes were wide, bright, sparkly, her mouth soft and pouty. Why did she have to look so pretty tonight? That wasn't going to help his case any. Exhaling, he continued, "Well—"

Amanda's startled gasp cut him off. Lifting a shaky arm, she pointed at the door. "That ape is the friend you need to help out?" She sputtered, trying to get out the rest of her thoughts. "How do you even know someone like that—that…"

Matt looked at Lexy again, wondering how she was taking this description of her brother. Her gaze went to her toes and she pressed her lips together.

He shook his head, half-relieved, half-amused. Overall, he was bewildered. Here he was worried about having to explain Lexy. "Amanda, why don't you sit down?"

Refusing to budge, she glared at him and folded her arms across her chest.

He shrugged and gestured Lexy to a forest-green leather chair, then he took the black one behind his desk. After they were both seated, with short jerky movements, Amanda gave in and sat primly in the chair that matched Lexy's.

"Amanda, this is Lexy," he said, smiling wryly at the belated introduction. "Lexy, Amanda."

Amanda blinked at the younger woman, a hint of surprise loosening her features, as though she was only just noticing Lexy. She seemed to gather her composure, sat a little straighter and nodded.

Lexy gave her a tentative smile. "Hi."

Matt cleared his throat. "The ape out there is Lexy's brother. And she's the one I'm trying to help. Not him."

Amanda's confused gaze darted from Matt to Lexy and back to Matt. "I'm listening."

"I know Lexy from college. Well, actually I was in law school and she was in college." He paused as he collected his thoughts, trying to decide what information to leave in without arousing suspicion. "Brad introduced us."

"So, she's an old girlfriend?" Amanda turned back to Lexy and sized her up with new interest.

"No," Matt and Lexy said together.

"We all sort of hung out as a group," Matt added. "Lexy had recently moved here from Hungary and we sort of showed her the ropes."

Frowning slightly, Amanda stared off toward the window.

As the silence stretched, Matt exchanged glances with Lexy. Amanda didn't look suspicious or mad...just sort of thoughtful.

Matt was about to elaborate when Amanda said, "So the ape's accent is Hungarian?" She darted a quick look at Lexy that was almost apologetic.

Lexy's lips curved good-naturedly. "Yes. Serge is only twenty-nine but he has lived in the countryside all his life and he still has some old ways."

"Old?" Amanda laughed, the pleasant sound startling Matt. "Try ancient." Then her eyes met Matt's probing ones and she sobered. "So, go on. What is it that Lexy needs?"

Matt nearly sighed with relief. To the point. That's one of the things he did appreciate about his fiancée. "Her family is visiting for two weeks. She has a daughter, and they think she's been happily married here in the States for the past seven years." He shrugged. "Basically, she needs a husband."

Amanda's eyebrows rose. "And that would be you?"

"Just for two weeks. A couple of dinners with the family. That's it."

Lexy fidgeted in her chair but remained silent.

Amanda frowned. "Why not Brad?"

Matt snorted. "Brad?"

She sighed. "Right. I see your point."

He was impressed at how calmly she was taking this. "What do you say, Amanda? Can we do this? It'll just cost me a little time, and you..." he paused, not wanting to set her off again. "Two weeks, Amanda. I'm asking you for two weeks."

Her forehead wrinkled in thought, and she slid Lexy a considering look. "You're not moving in, are you?"

Lexy flushed and her gaze darted to Matt before she murmured, "I have my own apartment."

"But her parents, of course, think she's living here," Matt added, deciding to keep things aboveboard, "so she'll be spending some time here."

Amanda leaned back in her chair, her lips pursed. "Hmmm, how cozy. So you're the husband." Her glance briefly skipped to Lexy. "She's the wife. And what, pray tell, does that make me?"

Matt shrugged. "The housekeeper."

Chapter Eleven

Lexy watched helplessly as Amanda stormed out from the study and Matthew leaped up from his chair to follow the angry blond woman.

"I'll be right back," he said. "Stay here."

"But—"

"Lexy, please," he said, holding up a hand, his face grim, before disappearing out the door.

She did as she was told. After all, this mess was all her fault. She should never have shown up unannounced. Except Matthew had said he wouldn't be home until late and she'd hoped she could give her parents a quick peek at his place, then somehow get them back to her own apartment for dinner.

Slumping down in her seat, she let out a loud sigh. She'd really gotten Matthew into big trouble now, just because she was as soft as a marshmallow when it came to her parents. Amanda did not look like the forgiving type. In fact, Matthew's fiancée didn't look like any type Lexy had imagined.

She was very stiff and proper, and her blue gaze could freeze boiling water. But she was beautiful, too, and wore chic, expensive clothes. Lexy supposed that was enough to make her Matthew's type.

Yet Matthew had chosen to help Lexy at the expense of Amanda's wrath.

The thrill of delight that shot through Lexy stunned her. She had no right getting excited over Matthew's allegiance. He somehow felt he owed her. That was the only reason he was helping her. It was nothing personal, no underlying feelings of desire or longing guided his decisions.

Lexy took a deep breath. She would do best to remember that important detail.

"I showed your father and Serge the bar," Matthew said as he returned and closed the door. "I hope that keeps them busy for a while."

Lexy started to grin. Just as abruptly, her amusement faded and she began pushing off her chair when she remembered her daughter. "Where's Natasha?"

Matthew laid a hand on her shoulder and urged her to stay seated. "She's okay. She's with your mom."

"But Natasha may say something she isn't supposed to."

"I doubt it. Your mother's rambling on in Hungarian and—" he paused, his face creasing in a frown "—she seems preoccupied with something in Tasha's hand."

"Oh." Lexy was careful to keep a blank expression. Now wasn't the time to explain her mother's legendary palm-reading ability…or what she planned to do with it for the next two weeks. "How's Tasha reacting?"

"Eyes wide. Lips zipped. We'll go rescue her in a minute."

"Okay." She glanced down at her clasped hands. "I'm sorry about tonight, Matthew. How mad is—will

Amanda—I hope I haven't made too big a mess for you.''

He sat on the edge of his desk, the crease of his slacks hitting her knee. After staring at her for a long, silent minute, he hooked a finger under her chin and nudged her face up. His expression was stern. "I ought to spank you."

She blinked. "What?"

"You'd deserve it, wouldn't you?"

"Matthew?" She scooted hopelessly back an inch.

His lips started to curve, and his finger left the underside of her chin to trail up her cheek. "What am I going to do with you?"

"Not spank me."

His gaze roamed her face, then came to rest on her mouth. "No," he agreed, "that would make too much noise."

Lexy's heart leaped at the sudden lowering of his voice. She swallowed at the way he continued to study her mouth. "What did Amanda say?"

The reminder of his fiancée was enough to distract him. His hand fell away from Lexy's face and his jaw tightened. "Not much. My guess is she'll give me the silent treatment for a couple of days."

"You'll try to talk to her, won't you? Maybe I could explain more—"

"No, let me handle it. The wedding invitations just went out. She won't be too quick to run to Daddy or anyone else."

At the mention of wedding invitations, misery swamped Lexy all over again. In a few weeks, Matthew would be Amanda's husband. It shouldn't matter. Lexy was only with him to please her parents. That's why she had gotten both Matthew and herself into this mess.

"Hey, don't start getting all maudlin on me now," Matthew said, tugging at her hand. "We have to figure out what we're going to do next."

She had no idea what *maudlin* meant, but she could guess. Swallowing back her self-pity, she started to rise. Matthew still had her hand, and he helped tug her up at the same time he slid off the corner of his desk.

There wasn't enough room in the small space between the desk and the chair for both of them, and Lexy ended up pressed against his chest. She grabbed his shoulders for balance. One of his hands cupped her waist, the other found her lower back. She stared helplessly up at him for a moment, her gaze trapped by the mesmerizing blue of his eyes.

The knock at the door was brief before she heard it open. Startled out of her foolish and fleeting fantasy, she started to move back. Matthew tightened his hold.

"Opportunity," he whispered before his mouth descended on hers.

Her breath got snared somewhere between her lungs and her mouth. Unable to escape, it fanned the fire burning and raging through her belly and thighs.

Her entire body went limp as Matthew's lips pressed insistently, slanting for better access, his tongue teasing the seam of her mouth until she was helpless to deny him entry.

She was going to slip into a boneless puddle at any moment, she just knew it, except Matthew held her firmly, molding the front of her body to his until his sex pressed against her belly, taunting her, weakening her...reminding her of how much she'd foolishly missed this man for the past seven years.

She had to stop this. Now. Before the seven years turned into an eternity of wanting something she could never have.

He's marrying someone else.

The sudden thought made her stiffen. She'd almost forgotten. Easy to do with the way he was kissing her.

At all costs, she would have to stay as far away from Matthew Monroe as she could. She'd handle her family. Tell them he was out of town...anything.

She pulled away just as someone cleared his throat.

Belatedly she remembered what had prompted the kiss, and with a very heated face, turned toward the door. Her father beamed with approval.

Embarrassed, she glanced at Matthew. He watched her, totally oblivious of her father, his eyes gleaming with something she could almost identify as longing.

Ridiculous. Opportunity, he had said. He was simply trying to offset any suspicion aroused by the earlier scene with Amanda.

Lexy turned back to her father, and addressing him in Hungarian in the vain hope that she could discourage his practice of English, she asked him if anything was wrong.

The corners of Boris Constantine's mouth lifted in the middle of his bushy black beard, and in horrible English he said, "We have plan." He took a lusty gulp from the half-filled brandy snifter he held, then wiped his mouth with the back of his hand. "Tomorrow we move in."

AS SOON AS they'd dropped off the Constantines at their motel and put Tasha to bed in Lexy's apartment, Matthew sprawled out on Lexy's uncomfortable couch and waited for her to put on the tea she insisted she needed. If it were up to him, they'd be downing a couple of strong Scotches about now.

He'd had no business kissing Lexy like that. None. No matter his initial intent, he was still too attracted to her.

From this angle in the living room he could see her bustle between the sink and stove, her finely curved backside swaying with each movement, forcing him to remember with vivid detail the kiss that had made him rock hard.

Cursing under his breath, he scrubbed at his eyes, trying to erase the image. This wasn't fair to Amanda. Or Lexy.

"Don't you want this?"

At the sound of her voice, he opened his eyes. Two nicely rounded breasts came into his direct line of vision and snagged his gaze. He swallowed, straightened. "What?" he asked at the same time his attention caught on the chipped yellow mug she was offering him. "Oh, yeah, thanks."

One-track mind? Him? Nah. He shook his head.

"Matthew." She squinted in confusion, her hand still extended with the ignored tea. "Do you want this or not?"

He took it from her and sat it roughly on the side table. "They can't move in."

"I know that." She started to sit beside him on the couch, gave him a wary sidelong look, then hastily moved to the recliner.

"What are you going to tell them?"

"I haven't figured that out yet."

"Why did they come up with this sudden brainstorm, anyway?" he asked, and waited while she thoughtfully sipped her tea. When it finally looked as though she either hadn't heard him or had no intention of answering, he ducked his head to meet her eyes. "Lexy?"

She looked away, then took another quick sip of her tea.

"Lexy." This time his tone brooked no argument.

She half shrugged, looking a lot as though she was hiding something. "Papa thinks you need help with the house."

"What kind of help?" Matt frowned. "If anything, our explanation is blown now that they see we're obviously not doing renovations."

She smiled brightly. Too brightly. "I come from a different background, Matthew. Family is important. When you have visitors, they are treated like royalty. You make room for them. You do not put them in a motel, even if there isn't much space. And Papa has decided there is plenty of space. But don't worry. I will talk to him again."

He sat in pensive silence for a moment, trying to ignore the spiraling guilt, then asked, "When did I give you the impression that I don't think family is important?"

Looking genuinely surprised at his question, she set aside her mug. "I know nothing about your parents or siblings, Matthew. You've never once spoken of them."

A sudden gloom fogged his mood, raised his defenses. "I was in law school, for crying out loud. You know how hard I studied." She smiled and gave him a small, indulgent nod. "And I wasn't exactly going to broadcast to them that I had married you because you paid me."

Somewhere deep inside he knew he'd intended to

hurt her with that unnecessary reminder, the way she'd just hurt him by bringing up such a touchy subject. But she didn't seem put off at all. Although her serene smile turned a little sad when she asked, "So, they are involved with this wedding?"

"Damn it, Lexy. We have more important things to worry about right now. Like how we're going to get *your* family off *my* back so I can get on with my unacceptable life."

This time his heartless arrow found its mark and color flooded her face, doing an admirable job of adding to his guilt. He had no business blasting Lexy because he'd been neglecting his family. They were important to him. But lately, he'd had a funny way of showing it.

"Of course." She reached for her tea again and focused on the ugly green mug. "But you have nothing to worry about. I'll take care of everything."

"Just like you already have."

She darted him a sour look. "If I have to tell them the truth, I'll do that."

He grunted with frustration. "Look, I'm sorry. We're both edgy."

"I know this is all my fault. I'm not trying to deny it."

Matt tried not to look at the way her breasts rose and fell with the deep, steadying breaths she took. She had no idea how much she was getting to him. That he was allowing such a strong physical reaction to her mere presence was solely his responsibility. It would be funny, really, if he were in a better mood.

In the courtroom he had nerves of steel. Facing an estimable opponent gave him an adrenaline rush as powerful as the first time he'd tried skydiving. But simply sitting in the same room with Lexy, watching her expressive brown eyes light with amusement or darken with wariness, the way her smile could brighten the room reduced him to a…a feeble old lady.

Why else had he screwed up with Amanda? The woman had a long, unforgiving memory. She was going to hold him hostage for life over this.

The rest of his life suddenly sounded like a devil of a long time.

Hell, he was a good lawyer. He didn't need Amanda's father's benevolence.

That sudden thought struck him like a well-aimed boxer's blow to his gut. Although he'd never lacked confidence, his future and his marriage to Amanda had paralleled in his head for so long that he'd developed blinders.

Brad had tried to tell him, but when had he ever listened to his laid-back friend? And why the big revelation now? Not that he thought this was truly a revelation. Or that he would change anything at this point.

"Matthew?" Lexy's soft voice whispered through his dark thoughts and brightened the room again, making it obvious his life was suddenly a mess. He hadn't gotten over her. "You look so upset. Please don't be angry with me."

He half smiled. The thing was, he hadn't realized how hooked he'd been in the first place. "I'm not angry with you." Her troubled, disbelieving eyes probed his. "In fact," he admitted, "I want to kiss you."

Her mouth opened but nothing came out. He heard her small gasp for air as surprise…delight…wariness chased across her face. "That can't happen again." She left her chair and with a shaky hand picked up her mug. "I'll talk to my parents tomorrow. They won't bother you about moving in again. Now, it's late. I have to be at work early tomorrow morning."

Watching her jerk suddenly, as if she'd just remembered something important she'd forgotten to do, he sat forward and peered intently at her. "I thought you cleared the next two weeks with your boss. Is he making you work the breakfast shift instead?"

"It's very late, Matthew," she repeated, looking pointedly at the kitchen wall clock.

The long hand was stuck on six. The thing obviously didn't work. Just like half the stuff in this godforsaken building. But she kept staring at it, anyway, as if she didn't want to look at him. And an unsavory idea formed in his head. "Do you have another job, Lexy?"

Briefly closing her eyes, she exhaled before meeting his gaze. "And what if I do?"

Good question. He shoved a restless hand through his hair, uncomfortable with the sudden powerless feeling that had him itching to do something for her. Lexy wasn't his responsibility. He had no right to get involved in her life.

"Mommy?"

They both turned to find Tasha standing in the hallway rubbing her eyes. Her bangs, poking up like tiny horns, made Matt smile. So did her pajamas. They were short and puffy with elastic ruffles around her thighs, and made her look like a little pink pumpkin.

"Oh, honey, were we talking too loud?" Lexy rushed over to give her daughter a hug. "I'm sorry we woke you."

"You didn't." Tasha yawned. "I was having a dream."

Lexy smoothed her hair down. "A bad dream?"

The child shook her head, a shy smile curving her lips. "A happy dream," she said, sliding Matt a peek before nestling her head against her mother's hip. "We were living in Popo's house and I had a big, beautiful room with a white-lace bed and a whole bunch of dolls from all over the world."

Lexy bit her lower lip and gave Matt a pained look before dropping to a crouch beside her daughter. She brushed a dark lock of hair away from Tasha's eyes. "You understand that we aren't really moving in with Popo, don't you, honey? We're just sort of pretending while Grandma and Grandpa are here, like when you play house."

Tasha made a resigned face and nodded. Then a grin tweaked the corners of her mouth again, her intermittent shy glances continuing to find Matt. "But I like my pretend room for now."

As petite as Lexy was, next to her, Natasha seemed like this unreal miniature-size person from a fairy tale.

He remembered how she'd sat on his shoulders earlier today, how she so easily trusted him, and he felt humbled. Protective. Not just toward Tasha, but Lexy, too. As though they were really his. And damned if the idea wasn't appealing. The unexpected feeling was startling, and scared the hell out of him.

"You're right, Lexy," he said in a suddenly gruff tone. "It's late. Call me tomorrow and tell me what's on the agenda."

He'd made it to the door, automatically testing the sturdiness of the knob he'd fixed, when Tasha said, "Wait, Popo."

He froze, both hating and prizing the deceitful name they'd instructed her to call him. The same endearment

Lexy had said she called her father as a child. "Yes," he said, the apprehension miraculously absent from his voice.

She crooked a tiny finger at him, one cheek starting to dimple. One little movement, and here he was—putty. The Constantine women sure had a way with him. He must have *sucker* tattooed across his forehead.

He glanced at Lexy, the fear he saw in her eyes puzzling him, making his steps falter as he approached them.

"Come down here," Tasha said when he'd stopped to stare at Lexy too long.

"Yes, missy, what can I do for you?" he asked as he hunkered down to her level.

She slipped a tentative arm around his neck and kissed his cheek. His late-evening beard must have surprised her because her eyes widened, and giggling, she rubbed the back of her arm across her mouth.

"Ooh, you feel like Mommy's legs sometimes."

Lexy gasped. "Natasha Grazyna Monroe, go back to bed this very minute."

Matt laughed, partly because Lexy looked as though she might blow a gasket and partly from nerves. Natasha Monroe had an unnerving ring to it. Even though he understood Lexy had used her married name for her parents' sake, actually hearing it struck a strange chord. Oddly, not an unpleasant one.

Tasha eyed her mother with mild concern. "What's wrong?"

Lexy pointed down the hall, her face stern.

"Night, Popo," Tasha said with a dramatic sigh as she swiveled around to trudge down the hall.

"Good night, princess."

"I want you asleep by the time I get in there," Lexy called after her.

Tasha sighed again before disappearing into her room.

Matt waited for Lexy to face him. "Remember when you used to get your razor mixed up with mine?"

She answered his grin with a small one of her own. "It used to make you crazy. I had to listen to a five-minute dissertation each time."

He frowned, balking at the exaggeration. "Yours was the pink one and mine was the blue one. How difficult was that?"

She shrugged. "Sometimes that was the only way you paid me any attention."

Dumbfounded, he stared at her.

"I'm kidding, Matthew," she said, and tried to urge him toward the door, even throwing in a fake yawn.

But she wasn't kidding. He knew that for certain. He felt it in his gut, in his rotten soul. God, but he'd been a jerk back then, treating her with flip arrogance, deep down knowing that she'd had a schoolgirl's crush on him. She'd been so young and vulnerable and he'd been a...bastard. Pure and simple.

For months after they'd made love he'd soothed his guilty conscience by rationalizing that she'd been the one who'd lured him into bed that night. But that wasn't true. Lexy had barely known what she was doing. And he'd been so turned on and stupid and eager that he hadn't even thought to use protection.

But drudging that all up now would do neither of them any good. Instead, he bailed out and opted for neutral ground and parting on an upbeat note.

Stopping briefly at the door, he turned and said, "You've done a great job with Tasha."

A faint smile touched her lips. "Thank you."

"Her father is really missing out," he said, his eyes locked with hers. And when Lexy's gaze didn't waver, he realized with a start that he'd been testing her.

And though technically she'd passed, still he could not quash his lingering doubt.

...standing beside at the door, he turned and said
"You've never been ... with Tasha."
A mirthless...ed his face. "Thank you."
"...Tasha is really irritating you," he said, his eyes
...to her with anger. And when Lexy's gaze slid toward
her bedroom with a what-did-I-tell-you look, he could
...what people especially since her boss might he could
not grasp her thoughts.

Chapter Twelve

Lexy watched helplessly as her parents continued to
pack their bags. Short of telling them she didn't want
them in her house—Matthew's house—she'd been unable to convince them to stay at the motel.

She slumped against the windowsill, making the
cheap venetian blinds rattle. Her parents looked up at
the noise. They knew she'd been edgy all morning.
But neither said anything. They didn't have to. Even
in their silence they controlled her.

It was both amazing and irritating to Lexy that even
after living as an independent woman for seven years
they still had so much power over her. The knowledge
also made her aware of how much her actions would
someday influence Tasha. The mere thought scared her
witless and she shoved it from her mind. She'd had
too little sleep and too much to worry about to try to
handle anything more than she needed to right now.
As hard as she'd tried, she couldn't get the desired
time off from her janitorial job. Her stingy boss had
given her only six days of her vacation time. That left
her with two early-morning absences she'd have to
account for if they were all under the same roof.

Which, of course, they wouldn't be, she thought,

and cast a forlorn look at her mother's attempt to zip her bulging suitcase. Any minute now Lexy would think of something to get herself out of this mess.

She sighed. She'd told Matthew she would take care of everything. What a terrific job she was doing. But no matter what, she wouldn't call him. She didn't want him running to her rescue anymore. In another week and a half, he'd be gone from her life forever.

Even now, though she'd brought this problem on herself, she resented the fact that she needed his help. For seven years she'd done fine, and now, all of a sudden, every time she turned around it seemed she was running to Matthew.

And each time he'd pulled through for her. But in the end, she knew it would once again be only her and Tasha. Matthew's plans did not include them. Nor did she want them to be included. She couldn't take more heartbreak.

A ringing noise startled her out of her musings, and she glanced around the room to look for the source. As soon as her father picked up her purse and glared at it with bewildered suspicion, she remembered the cell phone.

Quickly she grabbed the purse from him before he either tossed it out the window or in the toilet, thinking it was a bomb or something.

"Lexy?" Matthew answered her breathless greeting with concern in his voice. "What's going on? I haven't heard from you all day."

"Hi, honey." She smiled for her parents' sake. Her mother beamed back before returning to the long black trunk she'd begun filling with trinkets. Her father drew his dark brows together and folded his arms across his massive chest, his gaze fastened on Lexy.

She upped the wattage of her smile, then nonchalantly strolled out the door toward the privacy of the parking lot.

After a long pause, Matthew said, "I take it you're with your parents."

She sighed.

"That bad?" he asked, the understanding smile in his voice both cheering and annoying her.

"Not really."

"But you can't talk, right?"

She glanced over her shoulder. Her father had resumed his inspection of the air-conditioning unit. He wasn't listening even if he could hear or understand her. "Right."

Another long pause. "Okay, then we'll play twenty questions."

Lexy frowned. He wasn't making any sense. She knew he had questions, but how did he know exactly how many?

As if he sensed her confusion, he laughed. "It's a game, Lexy, also an expression. It means that I'll do the talking and you just have to answer yes or no."

She covered the mouthpiece in time to muffle her sigh of frustration. She didn't want to talk to Matthew right now. If she did, she might cave in and ask for his help. And she'd already depended upon him too much.

"Lexy?"

"Yes."

"Did you talk to them?"

"Yes."

"Do they understand that they have to stay at the motel?"

She hesitated as her father carried two suitcases out

onto the sidewalk near where she was standing. He took his time unloading while pinning her with a probing stare. She flashed him a reassuring smile, cleared her throat as he turned away, then replied with a shaky "Yes."

"And they have no problem with that?"

"No."

"Did you tell them that I would be out of town for a while?"

"Yes," she said quickly. Although she hadn't actually gotten that far yet, that was going to be an easy fib.

"So everything is under control?"

"Yes," she said, and plugged one ear when Serge slammed his nearby door. He placed a battered vinyl suitcase outside before giving her an enthusiastic wave, then entered her parents' room with a booming greeting.

"You're sure?"

She bristled at the skepticism in Matthew's voice, no matter that she was lying through her teeth. "Of course."

Seconds later, Serge and their father carried out the black trunk, both men showing the strain of its weight. They set it down with a loud thud only three feet from her.

How the heck did they think they were going to get that thing anywhere? How had they gotten it this far? As soon as they turned back toward the room, Lexy sank down on one corner of the second-generation trunk, her entire body sagging with despair.

"So I guess I don't need to worry about a thing," he said with an odd and cocky smugness that she would cheerfully love the opportunity to erase.

"That's right." She was going to hell for all this deception. No. She was already there. Closing her eyes, she began to lean back, but feeling only air, she remembered where she was and straightened just in time. "Is that all, *honey?*"

He laughed.

Behind her, Serge yelled something to Danica in the next room, which could probably be heard halfway down the block. Lexy covered her unoccupied ear, and in the other, she heard Matthew laugh again.

He sounded strange, not just because of the phone connection, but because his tone was a little too relaxed for him to be at his office, where she assumed he was. His work voice was brief, no-nonsense. Right now he sounded sort of...

She glanced with alarm at her watch. It was only noon. She frowned. "Where are—you're not at a bar, are you?"

He snorted. "Nope. Look across the street."

With an instant feeling of doom, Lexy reluctantly raised her gaze. Squinting into the sun's glare, she immediately saw Matthew's late-model BMW. He stuck out a hand and waved.

"WHAT WERE YOU planning on doing with them?" Matt asked when he finally got tired of Lexy's silent treatment. If he didn't know better, he would have thought he'd committed some grievous crime instead of having just bailed her out.

"Would you keep your voice down?" she demanded, and jerked a pair of shorts out of the paper sack she'd stashed in the corner of his bedroom.

"Your parents can't hear me. Their room is on the other side of Tasha's, and the whole clan is too busy unpacking, anyway.'' He frowned at the torn sack. ''I emptied out two drawers for you. You might as well use them.''

She fisted the shorts into a ball and threw them back in the sack. They had to be pretty brief for her to have been able to wad them up that small, and he regretted that he'd interrupted her from putting them on.

''I can't stay here,'' she said. ''I can't share this room with you.''

''Ah, so that's what's eating you.'' His nod of understanding was met with a murderous glare. ''What? I'm only trying to help.''

''Well...'' She put up a hand as she pushed past him. ''Just don't.''

Cocking his head to the side, he turned to track her movement. ''Excuse me?''

''I had everything under control.''

''Sure, that was obvious.''

She spun back toward him. ''What were you doing spying on me, anyway?''

''Mrs. Hershey told me she thought you could use my help.''

''Mrs. Hershey?'' Lexy stared back in openmouthed surprise. ''She called you?''

''No, I went to your apartment looking for you, and when she heard me knocking she came out and told me where you were and what was going on.''

''Liar. She didn't know what was going on.''

Matt lifted one deliberate brow.

Lexy's gaze flitted away. ''Don't look at me like that. I wasn't lying exactly. I just hadn't put my plan into action yet.''

''Which was?''

''Quit quizzing me, Matthew.'' Her entire body

shuddered as she turned to pick up the tie he'd discarded on the bed. She started smoothing it with short, nervous strokes.

"Lexy." He took the tie from her and tossed it over his suit jacket hanging on the mahogany valet sitting in the corner. "Come here."

When she wouldn't budge, he grasped her hands and gently tugged her toward him. Her gaze lifted and widened, and she stopped about a foot away, ignoring the extra tug he gave. Wary tension radiated from her eyes down to her fingertips, but she said nothing.

"If you're worried that your being here will make trouble for me with Amanda, that's not necessary. She left for a New York shopping trip this morning. That's her way of coping with stress. I talked to her before she left. She'll be fine."

Lexy's disbelieving eyes stayed glued to his, and he felt the strong urge to confess that he didn't give a flip what Amanda thought, anyway. It was obvious that humiliation was his fiancée's concern, not their relationship. She'd all but thrown that sorry fact in his face. Not that she'd had to.

"Look, Lexy, I'm going to sleep on the floor for tonight. You'll have the bed all to yourself. After tonight, our plan to let them believe I'm out of town could still work. I can move in with Brad, and you—"

"No, Matthew." She jerked back, but when he wouldn't let go of her hands, she ended up bouncing back against him, her right palm landing over his left nipple. Timidly, she withdrew her hand, and with a small flutter it landed near her throat. "Sorry."

"What are you objecting to?" he asked, trying to concentrate on the problem rather than the blood racing to his groin. Her sweet feminine heat was making a mockery of his thought process. If he had an ounce of sense left, he'd let her go, let her put some distance between them. That's what she wanted, too.

Or had wanted.

Right now her eyes were pools of warm, melted chocolate, reflecting his own desire and longing. This situation they were in was both vulnerable and volatile. One of them had to be smart. God help him, he hoped she at least had it in her.

"I can't let you keep rescuing me like this," she said finally, blinking, then looking at a spot near his shoulder. "It isn't…"

"Good for my inflated ego?" he asked, his mouth curving in a teasing grin.

"Good for me," she said, her serious and earnest eyes meeting his once more. "Tasha depends on me, Matthew. I have to depend on myself. I've managed for seven years. I don't want to change that."

What she was saying was she didn't need him. Fine. He didn't want to be in the picture. He had his career to think about.

And of course, Amanda.

"I understand," he said, shrugging and turning toward the sliding glass doors that led to the balcony off his bedroom. He'd had the master bedroom made larger than the original plan, and now he used every bit of extra space to put some distance between them. Not that it mattered. Emotionally, Lexy had already accomplished that quite effectively.

He looked out the glass doors and watched the oscillating sprinkler fan water over the emerald-green backyard while he listened to Lexy start to move around the bedroom again. The late-afternoon sun reflected off the droplets of moisture making them look like a sea of glittering diamonds.

Like the one sitting on Amanda's finger. The two-carat number she'd insisted upon and he'd gladly given in exchange for his career. At the time, it had seemed like a fair trade. Amanda would be marrying a husband who had money and status in the community. And Matt would be guaranteed a secure position with her daddy's prestigious law firm. For all their combined money and social climbing, they were both pretty pathetic, depending on each other for security. While Lexy held two jobs, was raising a child, going to school and depending on herself.

Matt shook his head, feeling the noose of humility tightening around his neck. Granted, he and Amanda weren't marrying strictly for convenience. They enjoyed each other's company, and they had a number of things in common. Although he was hard pressed to come up with anything off the cuff.

In fact, all he could think about was whether his career had been worth losing someone as loving and giving as Lexy.

LEXY FINISHED putting her things in order, at least enough so that it looked as though she actually lived in Matthew's house. He'd gone out about an hour ago, claiming he needed to run a few errands. He'd been silent and moody until he left.

She figured she knew what was bothering him. He thought she didn't need him. He was wrong. Lexy's problem was that she didn't *want* to need him. Something she was dangerously close to doing.

He was like a magician, coming up with answers when she was too frazzled to add one plus one, and then making everything run smoothly, seemingly without effort. Too many people to fit in his car? No problem. He rented a station wagon. When the trunk proved too long for the rental car, he had a driver and truck pick up her family's luggage. He was very good at providing material things, Lexy thought irritably. But that's where his generosity stopped. In a way, she pitied Amanda. Matthew had still not learned to give with his heart.

The noise volume beyond the bedroom was reaching a worrisome level, and Lexy smoothed back her hair and tugged down the hem of her shorts before leaving the room to investigate. Natasha was still at ballet class so she knew her daughter wasn't the problem. Besides, Tasha knew better than to create such a commotion, something Lexy feared her older brother hadn't learned. She cringed when his voice rose above the crinkling of paper and the tinkling of too many chimes, and hoped Matthew's neighbors had a good sense of humor. But when she heard the nostalgic jingle of a tambourine, she had to smile.

Rounding the corner into the living room, she stopped, then covered her mouth in horror at the transformation of Matthew's formerly elegant black, white and gold decor.

She blinked, trying to rid herself of the image. Maybe she was hallucinating, or summoning a childhood memory. But no matter how much she blinked or squinted, the dreadful scene remained stubbornly real.

Sitting on the glass coffee table were two rows of ugly plastic model ships in a choice of neon green or tomato red. Across the custom-made raw-silk white sofa lay several rolls of cheap, colorfully woven Turk-

ish rugs, wiry threads straggling from the poor crafts-
manship. From an original sculpture in the corner hung
dozens of silver and gold balloons still limp from lack
of helium tangled with beaded necklaces, and littering
Matthew's thick, pristine white carpet were bright orange inflatable toy lobsters.

A lump of hysteria blocked Lexy's throat as she
watched her mother pull more stuff out of the trunk.
Matthew was going to have a heart attack when he got
home.

Lexy opened her mouth to stop her mother, but no
words came. Instead, guilt swarmed her like bees
teeming a hive. This was how her family made their
living. Many hours spent standing on street corners,
peddling souvenirs, had helped pay for her American
education. What could she say to them now? Especially when she knew how much this visit had cost
them.

The sound of the front door opening sent a fresh
wave of panic crashing over her, and she was relieved
to see Serge and not Matthew open the door.

"Greetings, family," he said with his wide, boyish
grin. After propping the door open, he turned, struggling with something behind him for a moment, then
lifted the front end of a grocery store cart over the
threshold.

Their mother's abrupt bark stopped him from allowing the oily black wheels to make contact with the
white carpet. He obeyed her command and left the cart
on the front stoop, briefly wiping his boots on the outside rug and joining them in the living room while
Lexy cleared her throat twice, testing her ability to
speak.

"Serge," she finally asked in a reasonably calm voice, "where did you find that cart?"

His grin was proud, victorious, as if he'd uncovered some abandoned treasure. "Left by the roadside."

"Not a parking lot?"

He frowned, then slowly nodded. "Yes."

"It belongs to someone."

"Yes," he agreed, thumping his chest. "Me."

Lexy sighed. "You found it in a store parking lot. It belongs to that store. No one left it, Serge...." Frustrated, she slipped into Hungarian, trying to explain, but was interrupted by a curt knock at the door, which Serge had left open.

They all turned to stare at a uniformed policeman. His stern young face glared back, before his pointed gaze swept the pilfered grocery cart and the assortment of junk littering the floor and furniture. Slowly, he returned his attention to them while reaching into the breast pocket of his uniform and withdrawing a small notebook.

Lexy quickly stepped forward. "Good afternoon, officer," she said, smiling despite her shaky greeting. "May I help you?"

"Yes, ma'am." He gave Serge a brief measuring look, and with dread, she noted her brother's typical defensiveness in the way he lifted one cocky eyebrow. "Do you live here?"

She swallowed, hoping Serge had the good sense to keep his mouth shut. Not that she was counting on the impossible. "Uh, yes. Is something wrong?"

"Could be." The officer pursed his lips, then using an authoritative pause like a weapon, he surveyed the room. "Where did all this stuff come from?" he asked, gesturing with a short jerking motion toward the lobsters and plastic model ships.

"My family brought these things with them. They're visiting from Hungary," she said in a pleasant tone. With a firm hand behind her back, she motioned a restless Serge to stay put.

"And the grocery cart?"

Lexy laughed and waved a dismissive hand, then opened her mouth to explain at the same time Serge stepped forward.

The officer took half a step back.

"Serge," Lexy and her mother warned at the same time, while Lexy grabbed a hold of his shirttail.

A moment of strained silence stung the air.

Seconds later, an eruption of excited Hungarian broke the tension and everyone turned to see Danica rushing down the hall, her long hair flying around her flushed face, her hands gesturing wildly.

As soon as she caught sight of the handsome young police officer, she stopped complaining about the radio she couldn't get to work and broke into a wide smile. Her movements slowed, her hazel eyes danced with possibilities.

"Hello," she said, walking straight up to the man and giving him her hand. "I am Dani. You are friend of Lexy?"

Clearly taken aback, the policeman froze at first. Then he blinked his dazed green eyes, took her hand and stared back helplessly. "Officer Calhoun, ma'am," he said without letting go of her hand. "Jimmy," he added, shrugging. "Jimmy Calhoun."

Lexy relaxed at the familiar scene. Even when Dani's chestnut hair was still in pigtails she'd always managed to charm anyone in trousers. Keeping track of her mischief had nearly become Serge's full-time job.

Serge!

Lexy spun around in time to grab a hold of her brother's giant paw before he physically extracted Dani's hand from Officer Calhoun's grasp. His dark eyebrows were drawn together in attack mode, and knowing what would come next, she threw her arms around his solid waist and vainly used her body to propel him backward.

Behind him, Grazyna snagged him by two belt loops and instructed him in stern Hungarian to sit down.

Taken with Dani, Officer Calhoun didn't spare them a glance.

"What goes on here?"

Boris Constantine's booming voice stopped Serge cold, and everyone turned to watch him lumber through the kitchen door with a bulging turkey-and-Swiss sandwich halfway to his mouth. Delaying the bite, he frowned through his bushy black beard.

Serge straightened. "This *officer* wants my cart," he said. "I found it. It is mine."

Lexy let go of her brother and laughed. Everyone transferred their gazes to her. "I thought he—" Laughing again, she waved a hand. "Never mind. Let me handle this."

"I wish you would," the policeman said.

Taking a deep breath, she turned toward him.

Except it wasn't Officer Calhoun's eyes she met.

Her gaze slammed into Matthew's stunned expression. "Yeah," he said finally, dragging his gaze away and scanning the room with a look of barely concealed horror. "I'd like to hear this myself."

Chapter Thirteen

Matt stared in disbelief at his white custom-made couch, hardly visible under the piles of junk. The original sculpture for which he'd forked over three months' pay looked as appealing and decorative as a department store clothes rack.

"I can explain," Lexy said.

"Who are you?" the policeman asked, and Matt turned to eye the man.

The young officer spoke in a firm voice, his stance rigid, his badge polished to a high shine, but with Dani plastered to his side the way she was, and his hand hovering tentatively near her hip, it was hard to take the guy seriously.

"I live here," Matt said, and returned his attention to Lexy. "At least, I think I still do. Unless we've been rezoned for a swap meet."

Lexy frowned in a way that told him she couldn't quite translate his words. She quickly summoned a smile and said, "Officer Calhoun, please, there's been a misunderstanding. My family only recently arrived and they don't understand certain things and—if we return the cart, would that be all right?"

The man sent an uncertain glance at Dani, who

smiled broadly then adjusted his collar, her head tilted at a purposefully coy angle as she studied her handiwork.

Figuring he understood part of the problem, and in the interest of moving things along, Matt said, "I'm sure Dani wouldn't mind walking the cart back to wherever it came from." He met the other man's probing gaze. "Then maybe after Officer Calhoun is assured it's been returned, he'll forget about any charges."

The younger man frowned in thought. Dani shifted her left hip until it brushed his palm. "Okay," he said. "I'll accept that arrangement."

Matt would have chuckled at the officer's poor attempt to conceal his eagerness to be alone with Dani if Matt weren't in such a bad mood. Eleven more days of trying to cope with Lexy's family was going to do him in.

They had already started talking among themselves in a barrage of Hungarian, probably trying to decide if they could trust this poor, innocent law enforcement officer with the little vixen. She ignored them all, preferring to keep her sights on her victim. Matt kind of felt sorry for the guy. But of course, the officer had already seen her crazy family. If he still chose to pursue something with Dani, he was probably as nuts as the rest of them.

It appeared that Lexy had the final word. The others started down the hall toward the back of the house with only one hostile glare from Serge and two uncertain, over-the-shoulder glances from Boris in between bites of his sandwich.

"Do you know where the grocery store is?" Lexy asked her sister in slow, clear English.

Dani smiled. "No problem," she said, and tugged on Officer Calhoun's arm.

Without another word, the younger man followed her out of the room and they proceeded down the short flight of stairs. Seconds later, he appeared in the doorway again, his face slightly flushed as he gave them a sheepish grin and grabbed the forgotten grocery cart from the front stoop.

When he was gone, Matt closed the door then turned to Lexy. "I have a feeling we haven't seen the last of him."

She folded her arms across her chest. "I said I would handle it."

He started at the defensiveness in her voice, then swept a pointed look at the chaos around them. "Yeah, I can see that everything is under control."

Blinking, looking a little uncertain, she hesitated before lifting her chin. "You love playing the hero, don't you? Just so long as the door isn't locked."

Matt took a moment to process her words, but they didn't make any sense. However, there was no mistaking her irritation. Tough. He wasn't happy about his living room looking as though a tornado had hit it. "Is that one of your Hungarian proverbs, or something?"

"It's easy to step in when you don't have to assume responsibility, Matthew."

This wasn't about getting rid of the cop. "Why don't you come out and say what you really mean?"

Her chin lowered. "I don't have anything else to say."

"You want to talk about the past, Lexy, is that it?"

"No."

He jammed his hands into his pockets. Neither did

he. So what the hell was he doing provoking her like this? "What is all this stuff?" he asked, gesturing toward the sofa, the buried sculpture.

She moistened her lips and dropped her arms to her side. "My father and brother are street vendors. They brought some of their merchandise to sell."

Matt took another disbelieving look. She couldn't be serious. People here wouldn't buy this junk. He couldn't imagine anyone ever buying it.

"Things are different in my country," she said quietly, as though interpreting his thoughts. "This trip cost them a lot of money...more than they have. They thought they could—" She shook her head. "I'll talk to them."

Uneasiness at the way she so quickly read him had Matt shrugging, trying to diffuse his thoughts. "You understand they can't just set up shop on the street. They'd need a permit and—"

"I'll talk to them," she repeated tightly, and started picking up one inflatable lobster after another.

Matt stooped to help her but she waved him away. She wouldn't look up at him, just kept tossing stuff into the black trunk near the sliding glass doors.

Was she embarrassed, angry...what? He couldn't tell. Sometimes he thought he knew her so well, and other times he didn't have a clue as to what made Lexy tick. So, she wanted to be independent. He appreciated that about her, but she had asked for his help, damn it.

They were both under a lot of stress. He was supposed to be gearing up for a wedding, not meeting his almost-ex-in-laws for the first time and having his house turned inside out. Thank goodness Amanda was safely off in New York and he didn't have to worry about her for a while.

This situation was especially difficult for Lexy. She wasn't a liar. In spite of this mess in which they both found themselves, he knew enough to know there wasn't a dishonest bone in her body. Lying to the INS seven years ago had been a huge emotional dilemma for her. Love for her parents and a strong desire not to disappoint them had been the only thing that had forced Lexy into the marriage deception.

And now that same capacity for love had forced her into his life once more. She wasn't happy about it, and if he thought for one moment she was, he was fooling himself. Sure, she'd admitted loving him once. But that sort of reaction or false sense of love wasn't unusual for a virgin, and her affection had doubtlessly faded long ago.

The reminder of what he'd done to her that last night stung, and he had to turn away. She wouldn't let him help her, and he couldn't stomach just standing here watching her scramble. Proud, independent Lexy. How much had it hurt her to ask for his help again?

He opened his mouth to say something, anything to bridge the sudden unease between them. No words came. He fisted his hands around his keys. Sometimes a fast car solved a problem or two.

"Think I'll head uptown to pick up Tasha," he murmured on his way to the door, ignoring the fact that the child wouldn't be ready for another hour.

MATT STARED AT his plate. A strange and pungent aroma drifted up from the unidentifiable mound and assaulted his nose. He glanced around the table at everyone else's plate. They all were filled with the same thing. At least they weren't trying to poison him. Maybe. He frowned. Why wasn't everyone else eating? And why were they all looking at him?

Grazyna Constantine beamed at him, her eyebrows raised in anticipation. She'd spent most of the afternoon in the kitchen. He didn't dare tell her what he thought this dinner looked like, so he managed a weak smile.

His gaze swept to Lexy on his right. She pressed her lips together, obviously trying to hide her amusement. Well he was glad something had snapped her out of her earlier defensive mood.

"What is this?" Tasha asked, her face scrunched up in a horrified frown, and Matt wanted to kiss her for asking the million-dollar question.

Having drawn everyone's attention, she lowered her eyelashes, a shy pink creeping into her cheeks. "Why can't I have peanut butter and jelly?" she mumbled to Lexy.

"Ditto," Matt muttered.

Lexy only grinned. "Let me explain what everything is," she said, addressing her daughter. "You already eat everything that's here, you just don't recognize it." She paused and glanced around the table, stopping to smile sweetly at Matt. "You all can go ahead. It's my family's custom to wait for the head of the house to have the first bite."

"Yeah, well it's my custom to know what I'm eating," he muttered, and gestured for her to continue. He'd muffled his words and spoken quickly, hoping the rest of them couldn't understand. He'd discovered that successful trick earlier today. He didn't want to be impolite, but so far all he recognized were the meatball things, though he couldn't identify the type of meat.

Lexy pointed to the pale tan-colored mound. "This is called *topik*, an Armenian dish." Her gaze flicked uncertainly to her father. Annoyance darkened his face. She gave him a small shake of her head and whispered to Matt, "My father is half Turkish, and he thinks everything was discovered in Turkey. My mother thinks everything worthwhile comes from Hungary. I like to keep the peace."

She cleared her throat, and in a louder voice said, "It's made from chickpeas, potatoes and—" She frowned. Either she was searching for the English word or she didn't know what the ingredient was herself. This didn't look promising. Her face cleared. "Sesame paste. Then it is made into a pâté."

Tasha gave her mother a dirty look. Matt liked the kid more and more.

Serge sighed with impatience, one hand edging toward his bread plate. Although how the guy could still be hungry, Matt failed to understand. In one afternoon, he'd practically eaten half a turkey.

"This," Lexy continued, pointing to the meatballs, "is made from ground lamb, and the *borek* here is made from eggplant. You like eggplant, Tasha."

"No, I don't," the little girl mumbled, lowering her chin to her chest and refusing to look at anyone.

Boris Constantine said something in Hungarian, his tone stern and abrupt. Grazyna gasped and made a tsking noise.

Lexy's face fell.

"What?" Matt asked when she didn't explain.

She shook her head, refusing to meet his eyes, brief sadness tugging at her features. "He thinks I'm not a good mother." Her eyes suddenly widening, they found his. "No, I said that wrong. He thinks I am not strict enough with Tasha."

Matt could almost visibly see her confidence crumple, and her obvious pain from the unwarranted criticism sliced through him like a knife through cranberry jelly. He calmly lifted the napkin off his lap, belying the anger that began to smolder. She was the best mother a child could have, and no one was going to speak to Lexy that way. Not even her father.

Under the table, she reached over and laid a hand on his thigh. "Maybe you'd like to take Tasha to the kitchen. We have lots of leftover turkey," she said, her eyes pleading with him not to make trouble.

After a thoughtful pause, Matt set his refolded napkin beside his plate. "Please," he said, nudging his chin toward the table, "everyone start. Tasha and I have a couple of sandwiches to make."

He gave her a wink, and she grinned as she hopped off her chair.

Boris and Grazyna exchanged puzzled looks. Serge's mouth curved with eagerness as he stuck his fork into his food. Dani glanced at her wristwatch with impatience.

"Please," Matt repeated in a tone that said *"now,"* before he turned to follow Tasha into the kitchen.

Lexy was a big girl. They were her parents. He had no right to butt in.

And he wouldn't.

As long as Boris didn't criticize Lexy again. Even if Lexy wasn't the perfect mother and daughter—which she was—Matt figured it was a father's duty to encourage and praise, not look for small flaws. If

Tasha were really *his* daughter, he'd be bursting with pride.

Matt yanked the refrigerator door open with too much force, and Tasha abruptly moved back, the smile vanishing from her face.

Their gazes met and he smiled an apology, hoping to coax the dimple back in her left cheek. It hardly took any effort, and he immediately felt his temper start to diminish.

She was such a beautiful child, with smooth, silky-looking skin, a thick mane of dark hair like her mother's, and clear sky-blue eyes. Matt chuckled. Lexy was going to have her hands full for the next twelve or so years.

"I want mayo and mustard on mine, okay?" Tasha asked, looking up at him, her face upturned, her eyes catching the light, the twinkle giving her a mischievous look. "But not too much mustard or it makes my mouth go like this."

Scrunching up her lips, she made a funny face.

Matt laughed and touched the tip of her nose, making her dissolve into giggles. She'd become comfortable around him, much more so than with her own grandparents. He wondered how she'd get along with his folks. She'd have them wrapped around her little finger in a heartbeat.

But of course, she was no relation to them.

That he'd momentarily confused that fact shook him, and he returned to the business of getting their sandwich fixings out of the refrigerator.

"Okay, we've got turkey. We have mayo and mustard and pickles and cheese and lettuce and..."

Tasha put her hands over her ears. "No lettuce or tomato on mine."

"What?" he asked, and slowly turned, taking a step toward her. Then another. "Don't you know how healthy that stuff is?"

She lifted her shoulders in a deep shrug, her eyes starting to widen, then sparkle with excitement when she realized what he was up to. Too late, she tried to make a break for it, but he caught her around the waist and lifted her into the air.

She let out a shriek, threw back her head and laughed at the ceiling, while her pink jeans-clad legs dangled in midair. It was a low, throaty, contagious laugh that had him joining her when Lexy burst through the door.

"Tasha?" She stopped, her head rearing slightly back. And then her lips started to curve. "What's going on, you two?"

"We're making sandwiches," Tasha said, throwing herself backward and arching her spine to look upside down at her mother.

Her sudden shift of weight took Matt by surprise, and he stumbled forward, trying to renew his grip. Lexy rushed forward and braced Tasha from behind. Oblivious to her brush with danger, the girl bubbled with new laughter.

Hugging her against his chest, he briefly closed his eyes and exhaled his relief. When he opened them again, Lexy was gazing at him over Tasha's shoulder, a strange and unidentifiable emotion gleaming from her eyes.

Or were those tears?

"I wouldn't have dropped her," he said in a low voice that managed to survive Tasha's giddy laughter.

A sad smile inched across Lexy's mouth. "I know."

Matt frowned. So why was she looking so...funny? "Everything okay in there?" he asked, glancing toward the dining room.

She nodded.

"Are you okay?"

"Sure." She started to back up.

Tasha quit laughing and grabbed for her mother, and Lexy let her daughter slide a slim arm around Lexy's neck. Matt slackened his hold, ready to release Tasha to Lexy. But the child clamped her other arm firmly around his neck, too, their noses nearly touching.

"Come on," she said, smiling and looking from him to her mother. "Group hug. Just like a real family."

Matt didn't dare look at Lexy. Tasha's plea did something funny to him, distorted his senses somehow. And Lexy was too close, the soft look in her eyes too tempting. He avoided her face and focused on the swatch of hair touching her shoulder. Light shimmered off the silky strands.

"What?" He poked a finger in Tasha's ribs. "Where did you learn that?"

Giggling, squirming, she pressed her petal soft cheek against his. "TV, silly."

"Tasha, don't call Popo silly," Lexy said in that soft, sweet voice of hers, and Matt couldn't stop himself from looking at her.

Their gazes met and held. Tasha was there, between them, yet she wasn't. Lexy's smoldering brown eyes mirrored his longing...his confusion...

She slowly lowered her gaze to his mouth, her lips parting slightly. Her tongue darted out to moisten the pouty center of her bottom lip. Wetness glistened in its wake.

It wasn't fair, her tempting him like this in front of Tasha when he couldn't act on the sudden and strong desire he had to kiss her.

But then maybe that's why she was playing this dangerous game. Because she was safe.

Or thought she was.

A slow, lazy smile curved his tortured lips. "We'd better hurry and eat our dinner," he said to Tasha, but continued to purposefully hold Lexy's gaze captive. "It's almost time for bed."

And when a dull flush colored his wife's startled face, with a great deal of satisfaction, Matt knew she'd intercepted his thinly masked threat.

Chapter Fourteen

Lexy glanced at the kitchen clock. How much more time could she waste cleaning the kitchen? The refrigerator, stove and dishwasher all gleamed from the muscle she'd put behind scrubbing them down. Even the toaster and blender had not a single smudge on either of them.

She picked up the sponge and took another couple of swipes at the snow-white countertop. It didn't matter that she and Matthew would be sharing a room tonight, she told herself. They were both adults. Besides, she would be sleeping on the bed and he'd be sleeping on the floor.

Which was ridiculous.

They'd share the bed. He could sleep beneath the covers and he'd sleep on top. Or maybe…

Her head was pounding so hard it was becoming difficult to think straight. She tucked the sponge behind the sink, washed and dried her shaky hands, then started to massage her aching temples.

"Ah, Lexy?"

She looked up to find Matthew standing at the kitchen door, trying to look innocent while amusement dripped from him like water from a leaky faucet. She hadn't even heard him come in. How long had he been spying on her? One of her hands fell to her side. With the other she smoothed her hair. So maybe he knew she'd been avoiding him since dinner. So what? He was particularly annoying this evening, and she always avoided annoying people.

"Tasha needs a good-night kiss and I need some translation," he said, pushing the door open the rest of the way and strolling into the kitchen. "Your father is trying to tell me something, but we're not quite making a connection here."

"Where is Serge?"

"He went for a walk with Dani."

"Together?" Lexy asked, surprised. Things certainly had changed. Getting those two to do anything as a team generally required handcuffing them together.

"That's stretching it. Dani insisted she needed air." Matt's knowing grin indicated he knew full well what Dani was really up to. "Serge followed a minute later."

Lexy cringed. "Did you tell him it's a crime to punch a policeman in the nose in this country?"

Matt sobered quickly. "He wouldn't really do that, would he? What's Dani? Twenty-one?"

She lifted a shoulder. "It doesn't matter to Serge...or my father."

He paused, frowning idly at the refrigerator. "Yeah, well I guess I wouldn't be thrilled with Tasha meeting some guy once, then going off with him the same night no matter how old—" His gaze met hers and he abruptly added, "If she were my daughter, I mean."

Lexy walked past him and headed for the door.

"Well, Serge and Dani are on their own. Did Tasha already brush her teeth?"

"Yeah, she's picking out a bedtime story," he said, following her.

"And my dad?"

"What, we need to read to him, too?"

Lexy laughed. "No, you said he wants something?" She glanced at him the same time his hand shot out to touch her. She jerked back in surprise, but his warm hand circled her wrist and tugged her to a stop.

"It's good to hear you laugh," he said.

"I laugh all the time," she replied, careful to keep her gaze lowered. He was filling her private space, cocooning her with his heat. She didn't want to have to look into his blue hypnotic eyes, too.

"Not lately. You don't want your parents to think we're having marital problems, do you? Come on, loosen up." His hand moved up her arm to her neck and he began a slow, sensual massage, his long fingers kneading the tense muscles below her nape. With his other hand he cupped her shoulder, his thumb stroking the underside of her collarbone.

In spite of herself, she let her eyes drift close. His touch felt so good. Not just because her poor muscles were in dire need of being loosened up or because she was so touch starved it was pathetic, but because it was Matthew who was sharing his heat, making her tingle with an awareness she thought had died.

"That's it," he whispered, "relax."

His voice sounded closer. Maybe too close. She should open her eyes. Tell him to stop. But if she didn't...if she just pretended that...

"Alessandra!"

Her father's booming voice on the other side of the

door broke them apart faster than a bucket of cold water would have. He pushed his way into the kitchen and stopped just short of running them over. He looked from her to Matthew, then back to her, his black eyes lighting with recognition, his beard-framed mouth curving with approval.

Lexy took a step back, smoothed her hair, adjusted her shirt collar. She knew she looked guilty even though Matthew was supposed to be her husband and there was no need to feel that way. "Yes, Papa?"

He cleared his throat, his brows bunching with the strain of trying to concentrate. "I tell Matthew we need a little *raki*," he said making a drinking motion with his hand. He glanced over his shoulder toward the living room before lowering his voice. "Is there not a *meyhannes* close?"

Shaking her head, Lexy chuckled.

"What?" Matthew asked, looking from father to daughter. "I thought he wanted something to drink, but when I showed him the Evian and wine he gave me a dirty look."

"You're half right. He wants something to drink. He wants *raki*. It's a Turkish liquor made from…" She waved a hand, helpless to come up with the English translation. Ah. She remembered. "Aniseed."

A disgusted look crossed Matthew's face. "Aniseed?" He faked a shudder. "And *meyhannes* is Hungarian for bar?"

Her father had been squinting in confusion at their interchange, but at the mention of a possible watering hole, no matter how mangled Matthew's pronunciation, her father's expression perked up.

Lexy patted his arm and said to Matthew, "Actually it's a Turkish word for…well, *bar* is close enough."

She shrugged. "Papa uses it because he thinks Mama won't understand. Of course she does. They've been married for thirty years and Papa has always used that word."

Matthew frowned, then nodded. He clearly had no idea what she was talking about. "I doubt he'll find *raki* here."

Again, her father's face lit up and he slapped Matthew on the back. "Yes, *raki,*" he said. "We go."

Lexy quickly translated in Hungarian what Matthew had said.

Her father's expression grew thunderously dark.

Matthew audibly exhaled. "How about some beer, or vodka?"

Boris Constantine shook his head, muttered something, then repeated, "We go."

Lexy sighed. "He doesn't believe us. He thinks my mother is telling us to say this and wants to see for himself."

"He's not going to let it drop, is he?" Matthew shoved a hand through his hair.

She winced in apology.

A smile curved one side of Matthew's mouth and he lifted a hand to her face. She froze, darting a look at her father's watchful eyes before staring back at Matthew. Surely he wouldn't do anything... foolish...in front of her father.

No, but he was going to do something...husbandly.

Bracing herself, she watched him lower his face to hers, amusement and something more intense glittering from his eyes. "Keep our bed warm," he said, then briefly touched his lips to hers.

Then he dropped his hand, turned back to her father and, sighing, said, "We go."

AT TWELVE-THIRTY Lexy put down her book, crawled out of bed and crept to the window. She didn't have a view of the street from Matthew's bedroom, so she didn't know what exactly she expected to see as she stared out across the semi-dark backyard, letting her mind spin fanciful tales.

The moon was full and bright and scaring the heck out of her. Bad things always happened during full moons. And by her estimation, Matthew, her father and Serge should have been home over an hour ago.

It had been rotten luck for Serge to have returned home when he had. She swore his ears must have perked up from three blocks away at the mention of *raki* because he showed up on the front lawn before the other two men could get in the car. Not that she believed they would find *raki* anywhere in the city, but knowing Serge, he wouldn't be happy returning home until he'd gotten into at least one "friendly" barroom brawl.

At one, Lexy returned to bed and pulled the covers up to her chin. Everything was going to be fine. They were probably just having a good time, is all. And that was really lucky for her. She could be sound asleep before Matthew got home, and she wouldn't have to worry about keeping their bed warm, as he'd so annoyingly put it.

She knew he'd said that just to taunt her, that she had nothing to worry about, so why was she making herself crazy?

She wiggled into a more comfortable position. Matthew's bed was firmer than she was used to, that's why she was having trouble sleeping.

The brief, innocent kiss he'd given her before leaving replayed itself in her head, this time lasting a little longer, pressing against her mouth a little harder. It hadn't meant anything. He was engaged.

Lexy turned her face into the pillow and let out a low, frustrated shriek. She pounded a fist into the mattress. He was a devil in disguise, and she wouldn't pay any attention to him. That's what he wanted, to get a reaction out of her, and she just wouldn't fall for it anymore.

She flipped over onto her stomach. Sleep. That's what she was going to do. In his bed. He could take the floor. The heck with him.

A faint noise caught her attention. She stilled, willing the crazy-making in her head to settle down, and listened to the stubborn silence. A minute passed and not even a floor creak broke the quiet.

She punched her pillow.

And heard something again.

This time she kept perfectly still, staring at the red numbers on the digital clock, hardly daring to blink.

Muffled laughter from beyond the closed bedroom door ruffled the silent darkness. An emotional tug-of-war broke out in Lexy's tightened chest. She was glad they were home, and safe, judging by the laughter. She was not happy about the hour, or the fact that she wouldn't be sound asleep when Matthew came through the door.

But she could pretend to be.

Turning on her side, she drew the covers up over her shoulders and closed her eyes, allowing only the slightest possibility for light to filter in beneath her lids.

She waited like that for a long time, trying to quell her impatience, when she heard a knock at the door. After listening for another second to be sure she'd heard correctly, she bolted upright, her pulse picking up speed. It couldn't be Matthew, could it? He wouldn't knock in front of her father or brother.

And if it wasn't him…did that mean…

"Lexy?" Serge's urgent voice on the other side of the door confirmed her fear.

Something awful had happened to Matthew.

Ignoring the robe she'd left at the foot of the bed, Lexy flew across the room and opened the door.

Leaning heavily against her brother in the semidark hall, Matthew let his light brown head bob twice before he raised it and gave her a lopsided grin. "Hi, honey. I'm home."

She switched on the light. He immediately squinted his bleary and slightly unfocused eyes, then ducked his head.

"Hey, turn that off," he said, a look of horror crossing his face.

"You're drunk." Lexy folded her arms across her chest.

"Who?" Matthew's head bobbed up again.

Serge laughed. "Stand aside, little sister," he said, and started to help Matthew into the room.

She opened her mouth to tell him he couldn't come in like that, then wisely closed it again without saying any such thing. Instead, she moved to the side and said, "Where is Papa? Is he drunk, too?"

Serge half walked, half dragged Matthew to the edge of the bed, let him go and watched him slump to the mattress. "No, he is making a sandwich. He drove us home."

"He drove?" Her eyes widening, she uncrossed her arms. "Is—is Matthew's car okay?"

Matthew's head lolled back and he gazed up at her.

The collar of his polo shirt was all messed up, one side tucked into his shirt, the other pointing up. "What's wrong with my car?"

"It is fine," Serge said, and gave his shoulder a small tap, sending Matthew sprawling across the bed on his back. "It is a very fast car."

"Hey." Matthew struggled to return to a sitting position and settled for propping himself up on his elbows.

"You want I should take off his clothes?" Serge asked.

"That's okay," Lexy said, and tugged at her brother's arm, urging him toward the door.

"Your husband is a very good drinker," he said approvingly. "Next time we find *raki.*"

Lexy looked at Matthew's goofy, unfocused expression and couldn't help but smile. She seriously doubted there would be a next time. As it was, Matthew was going to have one heck of a headache tomorrow. She only hoped that he didn't have an early-morning appointment.

"Good night, Serge," she said, and gave her brother a final push out the door.

After clicking it shut, she turned to Matthew, her hands on her hips, wondering what she should do with him. He looked comfortable enough, and she figured she only need remove his shoes. If he stayed put, there would still be room on the bed for her.

"My car is okay, isn't it?" he asked, still propped on his elbows.

"Yes, Matthew," she answered patiently, only half blaming him for this condition. She never should have trusted her father and brother. They had enormous capacities for both food and alcohol and a childish fondness for daring other men to keep up. "Can you take your shoes off?"

"Sure." He tried to look at his feet, and when he couldn't see them, he kicked one leg up and nearly toppled over the side of the mattress.

"Wait." She hurried to his side and used her shoulder to nudge him closer to the center of the bed.

He circled his arms around her and, with surprising strength, hauled her atop him.

She squinted suspiciously at him. He didn't look like he was faking his tipsy condition. Besides, why would he do that?

"Hi, honey," he said, stroking her back, letting his palm drift too close to her rear end.

Rolling to the left, she ended up alongside him. "How many fingers am I holding up?" she asked.

He narrowed his gaze on her raised hand. "Three."

Okay, so he'd gotten the number correct. She didn't know what that proved, except she'd seen someone perform that test on TV when she was first learning English and it had somehow impressed her.

Matthew took ahold of her hand and brought the three fingers to his lips. He slipped the first one into his mouth and sucked the tip.

Startled, she tried to jerk her hand away.

But his hold was firm and not at all unpleasant, and he managed to slip the second finger into his mouth, as well.

Her pulse raced…then thudded when he released her. She started to draw back, but he shackled her wrist with strong unyielding fingers, stretching her arm out so that her body angled forward and her face was forced close to his.

"Did you miss me?" he asked.

Suspicion once again nibbled at her. "You're drunk."

"Not drunk," he said, his breath surprisingly minty smelling as it caressed her chin. "Feeling no pain, maybe."

"You still don't know what you're doing," she said, and hoped he was at least too intoxicated to notice her breathlessness.

"You wanna bet?" Smiling, he inched forward, his mouth aiming for hers.

He missed his target by an inch.

Lexy reared back, laughing, half-glad, half-disappointed.

"Hey," he said, letting his arm down but retaining his hold on her wrist so that she was trapped with her left breast pressed to his chest. "Let me try that again."

She wasn't doubtful of his condition anymore. In another minute he'd probably be fast asleep, and tomorrow he was going to have a foggy recollection of the night's events and a huge headache.

"I'll tell you what," she said, confident in her assumption. "If you still want to, we'll try tomorrow."

Matthew frowned. "What's wrong with right now?"

Lexy sighed. "You're seven years too late, Matthew. You're getting married, remember?"

He started to slowly shake his head. "It's not going to work. Amanda isn't the one..." He trailed off into a yawn, his eyelids drooping.

Lexy bit her lip, briefly closing her eyes. She shouldn't be listening to his drunken ramblings. He wasn't making sense. He was confusing her, feeding a small hope she couldn't encourage. "Go to sleep," she whispered.

"Hmm?" Matthew's eyes were closed, but he brought his free hand up to stroke her back. When his palm began to mold the curve of her buttocks, he smiled slowly. "You feel good, honey."

"Matthew, this is wrong," she said, struggling to keep her eyes open, fighting against the fiery sensations his touch was igniting.

Her mouth grew dry as awareness rippled down her spine. A pulsing heat flared where it had no business flaring. She squirmed, hoping to break contact, but the movement caused increased friction against her breast, making her go limp with helpless longing.

"Oh, Matthew," she said, sighing when he nuzzled her neck, taking tiny nips with his teeth. His tongue touched her earlobe.

She was the one who was going to have to put a stop to this, she reminded herself, and turned her head so he could have better access. And she would in just…a moment…or two.

A soft moan escaped her lips. Matthew had an amazing tongue. It had gotten much better with age.

Taking a deep breath, she summoned every ounce of willpower she possessed and pushed slightly away.

Matthew made a low, sexy noise deep in his throat and lifted his lids. When their eyes met, the corners of his mouth slowly curved in an even sexier smile.

"You smell good, Lexy. You always smell good," he said, trying to kiss her.

She resisted…barely. "Go to sleep, Matthew. I'm serious."

Letting out a frustrated groan, he slumped back

against the mattress and gazed at her through hooded eyes.

Telling herself she shouldn't feel disappointed that he'd given up, she twisted her hand to break loose from his grasp. Instead of releasing her, he tugged her toward him. She fell forward, her hand landing on his chest, her palm cupping the area over his heart.

Her face hovered above his by a mere two inches. He lifted his head and lightly bit her chin. "Closer," he whispered, and she realized he was trying to get to her mouth.

She was tempted to move that extra inch or two. Lord, she was tempted. But it wasn't right and it wasn't smart. Their arrangement was difficult enough, and they had another ten days left to share a bedroom, to share their lives. And kissing him was a complication she wasn't sure she could handle.

When it became obvious that she had no intention of moving, Matthew sighed and sank back again, then yawned. He moved his hand to cover the one she left resting on his chest.

"Ah, Lex," he mumbled in a sleepy voice. "You already have my heart, honey. You always have."

She blinked, suddenly feeling a little drunk herself. His mutterings were crazy words that meant nothing, she reminded herself. Words spilled from a bottle of liquor. She would be a fool to listen to them, to let them inspire any hope.

She closed her eyes because gazing into Matthew's earnest blue ones was too painful, too foolish....

And she was too sensible, too realistic to think anything had changed between them.

Yet how could he say these things? Matthew was not the type of man to betray the woman he loved.

Did he not love Amanda? He had married once before for money. Could he…

She discarded the thought. She was too confused and weary to think about it anymore.

After taking several deep breaths and forcing herself to calm down, she opened her eyes again.

Matthew was asleep.

She watched with a mixture of relief and sadness as his chest rose and fell, as his lower lip vibrated slightly from his deep, inebriated slumber.

His grip around her wrist had loosened, and with one small twist she could easily free herself. She didn't. Instead, she shifted her body so that it stretched out alongside his relaxed form. Then she lowered her head and pressed her cheek to his heart. For a moment she was going to pretend what Matthew had told her was true, that she was the woman he wanted. But only for that one moment, she promised herself. To linger would be dangerous.

Because if she were to be truly honest, Lexy would have to admit that she was still very much in love with Matthew Monroe.

Chapter Fifteen

Matt missed Lexy. He missed Tasha, too. And it had nothing to do with the fact that Brad was getting on his nerves.

To be fair, he knew he hadn't been Brad's favorite person during the past three days, either. It had been too long since either of them had had to put up with a roommate.

He picked up the phone to dial his friend's office when he saw Brad hurrying through the lobby toward the elevator. Matt jumped up from his chair, missed creaming his thigh on the corner of his desk by half an inch and caught up with his friend just as he was about to enter the elevator.

"You going to lunch?" Matt asked.

Brad sighed. "No offense, but I've seen enough of you this week."

"Then you'll be glad to know I'm moving out." Matt tossed him a crumpled ten-dollar bill. "You going by Dino's?" he asked, to which Brad nodded. "Get me a pastrami sandwich on rye."

The elevator quickly filled up with passengers, and someone called for Brad to hurry and board, but he waved them on and turned to Matt as the doors closed.

"How can you move out? I thought you and Lexy told her family that you'd be out of town for a week."

Matt shrugged. "So I came back early."

"Why?"

"I don't want to talk about it out here," Matt said, glancing around to see if anyone was listening. In fact, he didn't want to talk about it at all. He was a fool for returning home early. Staying at Brad's place while the Constantines were still here was the perfect solution.

Except he missed Lexy. Damn it.

Brad followed him back to his office. "You miss her, don't you?"

"Who?"

"Yup. I knew it." He closed the door behind him and gave Matt an irritating, know-it-all grin. "It was bound to happen."

"If I want a shrink, I'll pay the two hundred bucks an hour. Right now I'd rather have a sandwich," Matt said, and sat at his desk. The was the last bit of re-action Brad was going to get out of him. Then maybe the pain in the butt would get out.

Brad chuckled and made himself comfortable in the leather chair across from Matt. "You should have stayed with her in the first place. Lexy's perfect for you."

Matt lifted an amused brow. "You haven't seen her for seven years and you know all this?"

"Has she changed much?"

Matt snorted, and considered threatening to stay with Brad for the entire week. Maybe that would shut him up. Then another thought occurred to him. "Is this about Amanda? You starting to think you missed the boat?"

Brad's jaw slackened. "You gotta be kidding, pal. The ice queen?" He laughed and shook his head. "You had me going for a minute."

Matt narrowed his gaze in suspicion, then laughed, too. Nah, not Brad and Amanda. What a mind-boggling concept that was. So why had he considered it for even a single moment?

So he wouldn't have to feel guilty about Lexy.

He wanted her. Desperately. Too bad getting drunk had to be what had opened his eyes. Even after three days, thinking of that whopper of a hangover he'd nursed for an entire day still made him cringe.

"You look like hell all of a sudden."

He scrubbed at his face, then looked at Brad. "I was thinking about the other night and how I never want to smell another shot of tequila again."

"That stuff will kill you," Brad agreed, shaking his head. "I still can't believe you did that. Even in college you never got drunk with the rest of us." He laughed, then added, "No, you wait and get plastered with your father-in-law."

"Hell." Matt rammed a hand through his hair, exhaling loudly. It still galled him that he'd pulled that sophomoric stunt.

The reminder brought on the same sheepish feeling he experienced every time he recalled that night. His memory was a little foggy after the third bar, although he did seem to recollect standing on a stage somewhere and announcing to the world and Boris how much he loved his daughter.

The vague memory taunted him, had made concentration impossible all week. He'd talked to Lexy twice since he'd supposedly been out of town. She hadn't mentioned anything about the incident. But of course, if they'd understood him at all, neither Boris nor Serge would have found anything unusual about the fact that Matt loved his wife.

His wife.

He stared at his friend. Brad was sometimes a little irresponsible about female relationships and tended not to take his career seriously enough, but he'd always been there for Matt when it counted. "I'm in trouble," Matt said finally.

Brad nodded instant understanding. "When does Amanda get back?"

"Tomorrow." Matt frowned, unsure what was meant by the question. "I'm not going to do anything rash. I mean, the wedding is still on."

"Man, you're nuts. I saw this coming long before you even put that rock on Amanda's finger."

"This has nothing to do with her."

"I know. You've never forgotten Lexy."

Matt snorted. "You're the one who's nuts. I hadn't given her a thought in years."

"Maybe not consciously, but tell me you don't see her resemblance in every single woman you've dated since—petite, the dark hair, dark eyes…"

"Right. And Amanda doesn't blow your theory all to hell?"

"She's the one you chose to marry. You don't see something strange about that?" Brad stood, shaking his head, his agitation plain. "Everything has always gone your way, Matt. You've had it all. What could you possibly be running from?"

Matt stared in stunned disbelief. Was this the same guy he thought he knew so well? "I have no idea what you're talking about. But I don't think you'll have to worry about the lunch crowd,'' he said dryly, glancing at his watch.

Brad smiled. "Perfect grades, beautiful women, a job at the best law firm in the city right out of school." He gestured toward the windows overlooking a park. "The second-best office in the joint. And let's see, you've lost only one case so far?"

"I wouldn't call it a loss," Matt said, his defenses triggered. "We simply didn't get the settlement we wanted."

Brad's smile turned wry. "My mistake."

Matt shifted uneasily. "If you recall, I almost didn't get through law school due to lack of funds."

"Even then you landed on your feet."

Matt said nothing. What was the point of this conversation, anyway? He leaned back in his chair and adjusted his tie, exhaling loudly.

Brad walked to the door, then turned back to Matt. "Don't get me wrong. You deserve everything you have. You worked hard. Nothing was handed to you. Because you're smart. That's why I don't want to see you do something stupid now."

Matt flexed his left shoulder, still saying nothing. What was he supposed to say? Brad seemed to have all the answers.

"You've been happy for the past two weeks," Brad said. "That alone should tell you something."

Matt stared at the closed door long after his friend had left. He should have told him to forget the sandwich. He wasn't hungry now. However, he was annoyed.

Part of what Brad had said was right. Matt had been happy. Happy every time he watched Lexy play with Tasha or cook dinner or help her parents with their

English. Hell, her smile alone made him happy. So what? Lexy was a kind, giving person without a mean bone in her body.

And smart, too. Even when they'd been full-time students she'd always made time to tutor others. For free, even though he'd advised her to charge for her time. She'd told him an education was too precious to put a price on. And now, in her mid-twenties and with a child to raise, Lexy was still after that treasure. Because he had taken her money.

The sudden onslaught of guilt was staggering.

And almost a relief.

Guilt. That's all he was feeling. That's what was making him want to run to Lexy's side each day, kiss Tasha good-night before she went to sleep, pick her up from ballet or make sure they had enough groceries.

And lust, of course, because Lexy was a beautiful woman. One he admired for her courage and independence.

He swiveled around to stare out the window for a few minutes, trying to decide what exactly he needed to do. Amanda was the biggest problem. His conscience ran a close second. He couldn't go through with the wedding. It was that simple. And that complicated. The truth was, he didn't love Amanda. He cared for her and they often had good times together. But love? He doubted either of them understood the concept.

This wasn't a sudden revelation. The truth had been smoldering beneath their ambition. He'd wanted job security and convenience. She'd wanted status and social invitations. And now Matt wasn't sure any of that would replace a family. Or love. Maybe they could. But he needed more time to find out.

Turning back to his desk, he reached for the phone. The solution was obvious. He had to unclutter his life. Give himself breathing room. As soon as Amanda returned, he was going to have a heart-to-heart with her. Then he was going to give Lexy back her money. All of it. No matter how devious he had to be to do it.

And then he was going to sleep with her.

Maybe then he'd finally get Lexy out of his system.

LEXY TOOK EXTRA time blow-drying her hair, then patted a small dab of vanilla-scented cream behind her ears and between her breasts. It was foolish to be this excited about Matthew coming home tonight. His reasons had nothing to do with her. He probably needed something from his study. But she just couldn't help it. She'd missed him these past three days.

He'd been awfully good about calling daily to see if she needed anything. Not that she would have admitted that her father and Serge were going through the refrigerator faster than she could keep up with buying groceries. That wasn't Matthew's problem.

None of this mess was, yet he was coming home early. And she couldn't seem to ignore the thrill his decision gave her.

She checked her watch and calculated he'd be home in an hour. That gave her just enough time to make a nice dinner...if there was anything left in the refrigerator.

Serge and Dani were arguing about something, their voices carrying far too loudly as she came down the hall. As soon as she rounded the corner she identified the problem. High over his sister's head, Serge held the television's remote control.

Jumping up, Dani flailed her arms in an attempt to snag the device while calling him a pig, a jackass and a moose in rapid succession. His only reaction was to aim the remote at the television, flip through two channels, then raise it again to a height Dani couldn't reach.

Lexy sighed. She did not want Matthew to come home to this. She looked to her mother for help, but her blond head was bent over her tarot cards, oblivious to her children's bad behavior.

It had always been this way, Lexy remembered with frustration. Some things she did not miss one bit.

Someone knocked at the door, and as soon as Dani heard it, she stopped jumping and ran her fingers through her long, tangled hair. She gave Serge a final sock in the arm before she hurried to the door.

Lexy didn't bother to interfere with greeting their caller. Her sister had had many visitors in the past three days.

"Hello," Dani said, opening the door wide.

The besotted deliveryman grinned broadly. In his arms were two bags of groceries and Lexy winced. She wondered who had placed an order. She wasn't sure she had enough money to cover it.

Dani crooked her finger at the man, and he stepped into the living room. Behind him, Matthew appeared, his hand shooting out to stop the door from closing on him.

Lexy gasped. "You're early." She waved a frantic hand at Serge. "Turn that down."

Serge aimed the remote at the television, but she could swear the volume didn't decrease.

When she faced Matthew again, he was staring at Dani and the deliveryman's retreating backs as they headed for the kitchen. "When did Kroger start delivering groceries?" he asked.

She shrugged. "Dani asked."

Matthew laughed.

It was a pleasant sound that made Lexy's heart a little lighter. Out of the corner of her eye, she saw her mother staring oddly at her. And then she realized what was wrong. She'd forgotten their pretense.

"I'm glad you're home, honey," she said to Matthew, and rushed to him. "How was your trip?"

"Long." He immediately dropped the suitcase he was holding and gathered her in his arms. "Hi, Grace, Serge," he said over her head, his warm breath gliding across Lexy's temple.

She gave him a quick hug and started to pull back, figuring she had done her wifely duty, when Matthew lowered his face. "Where do you think you're going?" he asked, his smile white and dazzling and awfully close.

With her knees suddenly as boneless as a jellyfish, she wasn't going anywhere. "I have to make dinner."

"How about I take us all out to eat and we spend the extra time necking?" he whispered loudly.

Lexy glanced at her mother, who beamed with approval before returning to her tarot cards. Serge had already resumed flipping through television channels. She doubted they knew the term Matthew had used, but the way he was holding her and ducking in for a kiss was enough to convince anyone this was a joyous homecoming.

She relaxed, deciding she'd let him kiss her. How much could he do in front of her family?

He hooked a finger under her chin, made sure her anxious eyes met his smoldering ones, then pressed his lips to hers.

A second later he withdrew, first his lips, then his arms.

Disappointment drenched her like a sudden thundershower.

And then he stooped to slip an arm under her bottom and pick her up off the floor. She let out a small, surprised shriek, to which neither her mother nor her brother gave more than a fleeting glance and knowing smile.

As Matthew carried her toward the hall, her mother called in Hungarian not to worry about dinner. Stunned speechless, Lexy hung on to Matthew's neck until they made it to his bedroom.

He closed the door with his foot and slowly lowered her feet to the floor.

"Are you crazy?" she asked.

"Must be," he agreed. "Everyone seems to think so."

He sounded strange. In fact, he looked a little strange, too. "Have you been drinking again?"

The hand he was raising stilled. "Low blow, Lexy," he said, then cupped her cheek. "I just wanted to look convincing."

Her breath lodged like a rubber ball in her throat. His eyes couldn't possibly have gotten bluer in three days. "A hug and kiss would have been enough."

He tucked a strand of hair behind her ear, let his thumb trail across her jaw. His gaze roamed her face as if he were studying each individual feature and trying to memorize them. She shifted uncomfortably under the scrutiny.

"I really missed you," he said.

"Don't, Matthew. There's no one in the room but us."

"I know." He tilted her face up and covered her mouth with his.

He was gentle at first, letting her get used to the feel and taste of him. But then his hunger grew and he teased and taunted the seam of her lips until she could hold out no more, and finally opened up to him.

She whimpered and clutched at his shoulders, fearing that she didn't have the strength to keep herself upright. But he had already taken care of that by wrapping her in his arms, hauling her against him so that not an inch of space existed between them.

With a sweet ache, her breasts crushed against his hard chest and her fingers dug into his biceps. His hands cupped her bottom, his erection pushing hard and hot against her belly.

He broke the kiss, and in a raspy voice he whispered, "Man, Lexy. I didn't plan it to be this way."

"We can't do this," she said, her breathing as labored as his. "Not now." She meant not ever. "You're engaged, Matthew."

He shook his head and started to say something, then stopped and exhaled. "Something has changed. I can't explain yet. Will you trust me?"

Lexy stared up into his earnest blue eyes, and heaven help her, she did trust him. He'd never lied to her. Even seven years ago he'd been up front about his career coming first.

But she was confused, too.

"Lexy?" He brushed her lower lip with his thumb, and at his subtle retreat, her heart rate started to slow.

"What are you doing?" She jumped when he

slipped two fingers under the waistband of her denim skirt.

"Kiss me, Lexy."

"But…"

"Lexy."

Their lips met. He loosened her zipper. Her skirt slid to her hips.

She tried to pull away, but his warm hand slipped inside her panties and she was helpless to do anything but stand there frozen, fighting for air as he found her heat. He stuck one finger inside her, then two. And to Lexy's utter amazement, to her absolute humiliation, she exploded like a Fourth of July evening.

"Matthew," she gasped, squirming when wave after wave of sensation swept over her. She clutched at his biceps, intent on pushing him away. Instead she clung to him, too weak, too embarrassed to do anything else.

He pressed his lips to her temple, his warm, ragged breath stirring her hair. Although he kept perfectly still, his heart pounded against her chest in a ferocious rhythm.

When she was finally able to straighten, she saw that Matthew looked startled, too. And then he smiled. She tried to look away, but he took hold of her chin and forced her to look at him.

Matt stared at Lexy, not sure what to say. Thoughts were swirling and colliding in his head at a dangerous speed. He hadn't meant to go so far. He'd had every intention of talking to Amanda first, to make things right with her. But just seeing Lexy again had been his undoing. And for that, his battered conscience suffered another blow. Something about her made a mockery of his common sense, his self-control.

She'd surprised him by coming apart like she had. Even now her eyes were dazed, her body weak and in need of support. She'd been slick and wet and so ready for him. God, she'd been wet. He grew harder and uncomfortable just thinking about how easy it had been to slide into her, and had to push the thought aside. He was going to have to wait.

In an audible gasp, her breath caught, and he held his for a moment, believing she was going to start sobbing. But her eyes briefly drifted closed before they opened again, glassy, unfocused, with a small, satisfied smile playing about her lips.

An aftershock.

Hell, she hadn't finished, he realized, his blood pounding, his temperature soaring.

He knew he was good, but he doubted he was *that* good. She obviously hadn't been with a man in a very long time. In fact, if he didn't know better, he'd think this was her first time since they'd...

But that couldn't be. She had Tasha. She'd been with Tasha's father.

Then again, there may not have been anyone else. As enormous as that implication was, Matt wasn't upset. Maybe because, logically, he knew the idea was implausible.

He couldn't possibly have been the last man—the *only* man she'd been with. This was his ego talking...wishing...

But it was more than that, he reasoned. Lexy still seemed timid about sex, untutored. Even the way she kissed was endearingly shy and sweet...as though she hadn't had much practice.

Still, that proved nothing. Realistically, all he had was his suspicion, one that had seeded the day he'd met Tasha, and had continued to grow in spite of his denial.

He gazed down at the confusion starting to form in Lexy's eyes. She was coming back down to earth, and she was going to be angry...panicked...he didn't know.

He should ask her right now, while she was still in a state of flux, ask her if Tasha was his daughter. But did he truly want the answer?

Before he could form another thought, he lowered his mouth to Lexy's tentative lips. He teased them open, took what he wanted of her innocence. Not until her soft, helpless moan did he know for sure.

He wanted the answer. But he wanted Lexy to give it willingly.

Because she finally trusted him with the truth.

Chapter Sixteen

When they returned from dinner and pulled into the garage, Lexy was surprised to see the lamps on in the living room. She was sure she'd turned off everything but the porch light.

She glanced at Matthew, something she'd rarely done all evening. He'd remained subdued through most of their meal, not inviting conversation. Now he was frowning at the front window, too, as if trying to remember if he'd left the lights on.

Behind them in the back seat of the rented station wagon, her father had begun snoring, her mother was humming, and in the far seat facing the rear, Serge challenged Dani to yet another English word game. Between Lexy and Matthew, Tasha had fallen asleep like her grandfather.

Lexy brushed the hair off her daughter's forehead and wondered if she'd sensed the tension between Lexy and Matthew throughout the evening. Her family sure hadn't noticed anything was wrong. They had practically inhaled the Chinese food Matthew had treated them to for dinner. But Natasha had been quiet, even more so than usual, nibbling only on a shrimp egg roll and not touching the chicken fried rice she normally loved.

Lexy herself had eaten next to nothing. The memory of Matthew's lovemaking still burned brightly in her mind, seared her mouth, her entire body.

And so did his unsettling comment. He'd said something had changed. She figured it had to do with canceling the wedding. There could be no other explanation for Matthew's forward behavior. And that unnerving realization made Lexy numb.

"I'll carry her in," Matthew said, and she looked up to see him reach for Tasha. "No need to wake her."

Lexy had been so wrapped up in her thoughts that she hadn't realized he'd stopped the car and everyone was getting out. Pulling herself together, she trailed behind them through the back door, lingering in the kitchen, telling herself she could get through this evening, that nothing had changed between her and Matthew.

Midway through her pep talk, Serge's raised voice penetrated the kitchen door and her thoughts. Sighing, she rushed out to the living room, wondering what her brother had gotten into this time.

At first she saw nothing out of the ordinary. Her mother trailed her father down the hall toward the guest room Matthew had given them. Dani was nowhere to be seen, probably already on the phone in Matthew's den. No sign of Matthew, either, who'd no doubt taken Tasha straight to bed.

Lexy pushed past the dining room table, her gaze scanning the sunken living room for Serge. As she rounded the corner, she saw pale blond hair spilling over the arm of the sofa.

She blinked. Surprise, guilt and shame seeped in to fuel the panic filling her lungs as she recognized Amanda. Towering over her reclining form was Serge, a triumphant gleam in his eyes.

"So," he said, thumping his chest, "you finally come to my bed."

It was clear Amanda had dozed off by the way she raised herself to her elbows, a faint trace of dazed uncertainty coloring her expression. The look of bewilderment quickly cleared and she glared at Serge.

"You're insane," she said, and struggled to a sitting position. When Serge reached down to help her, she swatted his hand away.

"Keep it down, Serge, you'll wake Tasha," Matthew said as he entered the room. He stopped when he saw Amanda, his lips parting in silent surprise.

"Tell the big ape to back off, Matthew," she said, patting her hair into place, her gaze staying glued to Serge.

"Your housekeeper wants me," Serge said, shrugging.

Amanda laughed, the sound brittle, disbelieving. "Like I'd want a bad tummy tuck."

"You come to my bed."

Lexy gasped.

Matthew cleared his throat. "He's been sleeping on the couch."

Lexy's attention left the dueling pair to stare at Matthew. She had not imagined the amusement in his voice. A hint of a smile lurked at the corners of his mouth. He clearly wasn't upset. As he would be if he were still engaged to Amanda, Lexy thought, a new wave of panic and hope washing over her.

A low, feminine growl drew her attention back to

the other two. "And you think I purposely lay here waiting for you?" Amanda narrowed her fiery gaze. "You are truly delusional."

Lexy doubted Serge understood that word. She wasn't sure she did, either, but Serge merely grinned and reached for Amanda. Obviously taken by surprise, she let him haul her to her feet, and she ended up plastered to his chest.

"Serge," Lexy snapped, her warning falling on deaf ears when he slid his arms around the other woman. Amanda gazed up at him, stunned into silence. Lexy clutched Matthew's arm. "Do something."

Matthew slowly shook his head, his expression an odd mixture of amazement and resignation. "Who would have thought it?"

He didn't look or sound at all like himself right now, and Lexy couldn't tell if he was angry or shocked or embarrassed. She was feeling all three. And ready to kill her brother.

"Serge," she said, starting to step forward, but Matthew stopped her with a gentle hand on her arm.

"Look at them," he said. "They don't want to be interrupted."

Lexy turned toward the couple. Amanda had quit struggling, although Serge's big strong arms were clearly not restraining her. They circled her in a caressing manner and her fists had relaxed until her palms flattened against his chest. Both excitement and longing flared in her eyes before she blinked and slid them a sheepish look.

Serge released her, stepped back and gave a slight bow in a way that Lexy recognized as his courting stance. "We have a drink now," he said.

Lexy opened her mouth to protest, but Matthew

tugged so hard at her hand that she stumbled toward him. "Amanda, Serge," he said, "would you excuse us for a moment?"

Amanda took another step back from Serge and shrugged in a helpless gesture. She looked confused and a little meek, an experience, Lexy would bet, that was entirely foreign to her. "Of course."

Feeling rather out of sorts herself, Lexy let Matthew hold her hand as she followed him to his room. "I'm so sorry about Serge," she said, breaking free as soon as Matthew shut the door behind them. "He doesn't know who Amanda really is and, well, many times ladies find him attractive, although I can't understand why, but I'm really—"

Matthew silenced her by putting two fingers up to her lips. "It's okay."

"You don't understand. You don't know Serge—"

"Hell, apparently I don't even know Amanda." He didn't seem the least bit upset.

Lexy folded her arms across her chest, the embarrassment over her brother's behavior giving way to the anger and frustration that had simmered inside her all evening. "I am ready for your explanation."

"You'll have it. Soon. I promise." He reached for her, but she jerked away.

"No, we can't."

He grabbed both her arms and made her face him. "There's not going to be a wedding, Lexy."

Her eyes widened and her pulse began to quicken, even though in her heart, she'd already known this was coming. Or maybe she'd only wished for it to ease her guilt and shame for this afternoon.

She broke away and walked to the window, rubbing the sudden chill from her arms. Either way, Matthew's decision had nothing to do with her. Even if it had, once he found out about Tasha... Oh, God, she didn't want to think about that.

"If this has to do with Serge, I'll talk to him. "I'll tell him the truth. He won't tell the rest."

"No," he said, and when she heard the doorknob, she turned from the window to find him opening the door. "I need to talk to Amanda. You get some rest."

He left the room before Lexy could utter another word.

She thought briefly about running after him and demanding he tell her more. She was sick of him walking away without giving her explanations. But was she truly prepared for what he might say?

She changed into shorts and a T-shirt and crawled into bed. When he returned, she'd make a statement by switching to the floor. No matter what happened between him and Amanda, Lexy had no intention of them taking up where they'd left off earlier this afternoon.

Her heart had been broken once before, and it had been hard enough then, being young, pregnant, alone, trying to pick up the pieces. Now the stakes were even higher. She had Tasha to think about, and Matthew didn't have a track record for sticking around.

Two hours later, Lexy lay wide awake staring at the ceiling. Through the darkened silence she heard Matthew's car start. She buried her face in the pillow, praying for sleep, not one bit surprised he was leaving. Again.

"THERE'S A FLEA market over at the old Sunnydale drive-in," Matthew announced at breakfast two mornings later. "It'll be open tomorrow and Sunday if you folks want to go."

Lexy broke two more eggs into the bowl. Serge had already eaten most of the first batch of French toast she'd made. She slanted a glance at Matthew, but catching her parents' bewildered looks, she quickly explained in Hungarian what Matthew meant by a flea market. They beamed at him.

"Maybe you can sell some of your merchandise there," he said, walking up to Lexy and putting a possessive hand at her waist while he leaned past her to snitch a strip of bacon. "If you're interested, I'll call around this morning to see if you need a permit or something."

His touch both annoyed and thrilled her. Since the night he'd left her to talk to Amanda, he'd paid Lexy little attention. Each night he seemed to work a little later, and each morning he was gone by the time she got out of the shower. Except for this morning. He'd lingered well past his normal time to leave for work while dressed in khakis and a sport jacket instead of his usual dark suit. And as curious as Lexy was, she hadn't asked for an explanation.

The truth was, she'd avoided him, too. She didn't understand the reason for his moodiness, and none of the possibilities she considered were encouraging. Although he'd said his talk with Amanda had gone well, that they were in agreement, Lexy figured he might be having second thoughts about ending the engagement. Even though that should mean nothing to her, it did. No matter how much she tried to quash the feelings, guilt, confusion, hope and fear converged on her at the oddest times. Like when she found Matthew staring at their daughter. Which he did often. Too often for Lexy's peace of mind.

She realized everyone was looking at her expectantly, and she took a deep, calming breath.

"That would be very nice, Matthew," Lexy said, meaning it. She'd explained to him that her parents had hoped to pay for much of their trip by selling their wares, and she appreciated his helping out like this.

He winked and brushed his lips across her cheek before retreating.

She momentarily tensed, her entire body tingling with his innocent and unexpected kiss. If you could even call it that. He'd merely grazed her skin with his lips and she was about to fall apart. It was pathetic and embarrassing and totally unacceptable.

Beating the eggs with extra effort, she started translating his words for her parents. To her own ears, she sounded flustered, but she received no reaction from him. He simply went to the refrigerator for some orange juice. Her parents talked excitedly to each other, making plans, her mother speculating on a palm-reading booth, as she cleared their plates from the small kitchen table.

Lexy took a deep breath. "I guess you can tell they accept your offer," she told Matthew.

He smiled, poured his juice, then gulped it down.

She watched his throat work, while admiring the clean, strong line of his jaw. He had a great mouth, too. It did miraculous things to her.

Nearly choking on her thoughts, she forced her attention back to fixing more French toast. Half the egg mixture had sloshed out of the bowl and onto the white countertop.

Sighing in dismay, she angled her body, hoping Matthew wouldn't notice her flustered clumsiness.

He handed her a paper towel.

"Thanks," she mumbled.

He gave her fanny a small pat. She jumped but held her tongue since her parents were still there. "You'll probably want to go with them to the flea market," he said.

She shrugged, glad he was getting back to business. "They may need translation."

He nodded. "I'll drop you all off. I suppose Serge and Dani will want to go."

She nodded, smiling in gratitude for his kindness. "Tasha has never been to anything like that. She'll have fun, too."

"No," he said. "Not Tasha. She'll stay with me."

Her eyes widened, the firmness in his voice making her uneasy. "What do you mean?"

"I'd like to spend the day with her."

She shook her head. "She stays with me."

"Lexy," he said, his abrupt tone earning her parents' attention. "I'd like to spend some time with our daughter. I was thinking of taking her to see my family." He spoke deliberately, clearly and slowly, and it appeared by their sudden interest that her parents understood at least part of what he'd said.

Panic raced through Lexy as her gaze dueled with his. What was Matthew doing? Why would he want Tasha to meet his family?

Lexy moistened her lips, then slid her father a quick look. Disapproval lurked at the corners of his tightened mouth. He did not like Lexy defying her husband, no matter what the discussion. Besides, why wouldn't she want their daughter to spend time with Matthew's family? Her father didn't know that she and Tasha had never met them, that they'd had no reason to meet them.

She swallowed. "Of course," she said, trying to smile. "What a good idea."

THE DAY OF THE flea market was overcast and gloomy. It matched Lexy's mood perfectly. Her family would be leaving in five days, and God forgive her, she couldn't wait for them to go.

She was tired of trying to be cheerful, of pretending that she didn't care that Matthew chose to sleep on the floor instead of in bed with her. Not that she wanted anything to happen between them. She didn't. Not now, not ever.

"Are we ready?" Matthew asked, surveying the crammed rear compartment of the station wagon.

Serge put his weight against the back door, then clicked it shut. They'd put all the seats down in order to accommodate the merchandise. Matthew planned to take Serge and their father to the grounds first to start setting up their booth. Then he would return to pick up the women.

Lexy looked on, holding Tasha close to her. She hadn't yet decided what to do about letting Tasha go alone with Matthew. She only knew that wasn't going to happen.

Serge called to Boris, who was rummaging through the refrigerator for a snack to take along with him. He appeared at the door, securing two chicken legs in plastic wrap. "I come."

Tasha tugged at Lexy's hand. "Popo says we're going to have bratwurst for lunch." She wrinkled her nose. "He says they always have that for lunch at the

Monroe house on Sundays, but I don't know what that is.''

She squeezed her daughter's hand so tight, Tasha winced. ''Sorry, honey, I don't know, either, but let's not worry about that right now, okay?''

Tasha's big blue eyes rounded. ''Why don't you come with us, Mommy?''

Matthew had just opened the driver's door. He looked over at them, hesitating, as though he were waiting for Lexy's answer. But he hadn't actually invited her. In fact, she'd gotten the impression that she wasn't welcome to accompany them.

''Mommy?''

She looked down at her daughter's expectant face. ''I don't know, honey. I don't—'' Her gaze drew back to Matthew as though she had no choice, as though he'd somehow willed her to meet his eyes. They looked fierce, intense. They seemed to know all her secrets. They made her shiver. ''I don't know if Popo wants me to,'' she said, still looking at Matthew.

Both Serge and her father had already gotten in the car and waited with impatient twitches. That didn't seem to bother Matthew. Nothing, in fact, seemed to faze him lately. He was often moody and preoccupied, and even now he let the silence fester for another full minute before finally saying, ''That depends, Lexy—'' he smiled briefly, reassuringly at Tasha before letting his cool gaze drift back to Lexy ''—on whether you want to be a part of this family or not.''

He continued to stare at her, unblinking, unsmiling, and, heaven help her, she received his message loud and clear.

Lexy reflexively tightened her hold on Tasha's hand.

Matthew was *not* going to take their daughter away.

DISMAL, MENACING thoughts clawed at Lexy for the silent hour-long drive to Matthew's family's home. He knew about Tasha. He had to know. Was that what the broken engagement was about? Did he want Tasha, but Amanda refused to mother another woman's child? Matthew had never wanted a family. But he'd changed in many ways Lexy couldn't ignore. He was more patient and responsive, and as far as Tasha went, he was never too busy for her. He always made time to pick her up from ballet or to study and praise her artwork. He acted like a proud papa.

Guilt cramped Lexy's stomach. Maybe she'd been wrong in not telling him about their daughter. Or just maybe, guilt was making her see things that weren't there at all.

Trying to stop her mind from racing, Lexy vaguely listened as Tasha excitedly pointed out the cows chewing grass along the roadside as the endless flat, parched landscape stretched from the city to the bordering farms.

As soon as Matthew pulled the car into the gravel drive of his family's small two-story brick colonial, an unexpected pang of homesickness vibrated in her chest. Not because this house bore any resemblance to the tiny two-bedroom cottage she grew up in, but because life suddenly seemed overwhelming right now. And this plain, faded blue house with its red trim sitting on acres of unspoiled land reminded her of Hungary and simpler times.

"Is this your house, Popo?" Tasha asked, a smile spreading across her smooth little-girl face, and Lexy had to smother the reflexive urge to forbid her from calling him that anymore.

Matthew smiled back. "No, it's my father and mother's home, but I grew up here."

"Did you ride cows?" she asked, her smitten gaze drawn to a herd in the neighboring pasture.

He laughed. "My father was a teacher. We didn't have cows or horses. Only a garden."

The front door slammed. Several fair heads poked out. Whoops and greetings were shouted as people in varying heights and sizes rushed from the house toward the car.

Matthew's sister Amy and her two children reached them first. By the time hugs and introductions were distributed all around, his other sister Bonnie and her three boys arrived on the scene.

"Matt." A tall, thin woman with a welcoming smile, who could only be his mother, stepped onto the porch. Drying her hands on her apron, she hurried outside to give her son a hug and kiss. Then she turned to Lexy and Tasha and held out her arms. "I'm so glad to finally meet you."

Finally? Lexy darted a look at Matthew, who'd said he'd explained her as a friend. He was smiling, really smiling for the first time all day. She put a hand out to his mother and was enveloped in a huge hug.

Everything was a whirlwind of noise and excitement after that as Lexy met two of his brothers and their wives and children and learned that there was one more sister whom Matthew's father had just gone to pick up. It surprised Lexy that his family was not unlike her own. They were loud and squabbled playfully and teased one another mercilessly. They were completely unexpected.

Once she got over her shyness, Tasha was in heaven, too, playing with all the children. There were two girls her age and a boy a year younger. The older ones stuck to Matthew, badgering him until he finally agreed to a game of football.

Watching her daughter, Lexy felt guilty and wistful and annoyed with Matthew. These children were Tasha's cousins, and Lexy felt like the wicked witch keeping her from them. But of course, she wasn't to blame. Matthew was the one who'd left.

But you didn't tell him about Tasha, a small voice said.

Lexy cringed and pushed the thought aside. It wouldn't have mattered. Matthew had been more concerned with his career than raising a family. He still was. Wasn't he?

"Lexy, save me."

She looked up to see Matthew stumbling toward her, half doubled over in pain. Her irritation instantly forgotten, she jumped off the porch swing and ran to him.

"Matthew," she said, circling a supporting arm around him, pressing her free hand to his damp, flushed cheek. "What's wrong, Matthew?"

His sister Amy, who was sitting on the first step, burst out laughing. "He's getting old and soft, that's what."

A grin twitched at one side of his mouth.

Lexy reared her head back. "Matthew?" He gave her a puppy-dog look, then broke into a smile. "You—you donkey." She shoved him away.

He caught her hand. "I wasn't kidding," he said, straightening. "Those guys play rough."

She sniffed because she really wanted to smile back.

But she was still upset with him and he probably thought he could coax a smile out of her any time he wanted.

"Come on, Lexy," he said, tugging at her hand. "Walk with me." She hesitated, and he added, "Okay, but you're responsible if those kids drag me back out there and I keel over."

Her lips did begin to curve then because she had the nasty and fleeting thought that that would certainly solve some of her problems. "Where are we going?" she asked as he pulled her across the drive toward a row of trees.

"You're gonna have to trust me, honey," he said, and something in his tone made Lexy shiver.

She still didn't know why they were here, why Matthew suddenly decided Tasha should meet his family. Every possible reason she'd come up with scared the heck out of her.

Maybe she was overreacting. She'd been very tired for the past week and a half. Maybe Matthew didn't really know about Tasha. She glanced over her shoulder, suddenly reluctant to leave her daughter alone with her cousins.

"She'll be fine," he said. "Her, uh, new friends will take good care of her."

Lexy held her breath and gritted her teeth. What had Matthew been about to say? Her mind started racing again as she thought of all the possible outcomes of this horrible mess she'd placed herself and Tasha in. Surely he wouldn't be thinking of kidnapping her. Lexy now knew where his family lived.

She was being silly. This was Matthew. He wouldn't hurt her or Tasha. Besides, he knew the law. He had money. If he wanted to take Tasha, he could.

Lexy mentally shook herself. She was being irrational, crazy, out of control. And she was depressing herself to no end.

Matthew stopped on the other side of the trees. He stared at her, his eyes dark with concern. "You look like you're going to explode," he said, forcing her chin up. "Anything you want to talk about?"

She jerked away and shook her head.

"You're sure there's nothing you want to get off your chest?"

She tried to slow her breathing, tried to meet his gaze. She couldn't. He was going to talk about Tasha.

"Trust goes both ways, Lexy."

"We'd better get back."

"You can't keep running away if we're ever going to have another chance."

Another chance? She swallowed a sob. "I'm not the one who ran away," she said, and turned to leave, but he caught her hand and pulled her toward him.

"Can't you forget the past?"

She let herself relax against his chest. Mostly so he couldn't look at her. She didn't want him to see the betrayal in her eyes. She felt the brief kiss he placed in her hair, and lowered her lids, wishing everything could go back to normal. What had seemed like a simple decision seven years ago was about to tear her world apart.

"See that stream over there?" He pointed past a clump of low-lying shrubs.

Relieved at the change in subject, she squinted against the glare of the sun, shading her eyes with her hand. "Oh, Matthew, it looks like a postcard."

"Yeah, it does, huh?" He half laughed. "I didn't think so when I was a kid. I used to skip rocks across it every day after school, vowing I'd get as far away from here as I could.''

''You did.''

One side of his mouth rode up in self-deprecation. He knew she wasn't talking about distance. ''Ever hear the American saying about thinking the grass is greener on the other side?''

She shook her head, but she figured she knew what it meant. ''Now you regret leaving?''

''No, but I understand the attraction to stay, why my father broke his butt and sacrificed in order to raise his kids here. I imagine there isn't much a parent wouldn't do for his children.''

Against her will, she met his gaze. What was he telling her? That he knew Tasha was his daughter? Or was he trying to trick her into an admission? She didn't want to believe that of him. And she didn't, really. But could she risk losing Tasha?

A loud commotion coming from the house had them both turning around to see the kids running toward a car pulling in the drive.

''Well, here come the rest of the troops. Come on,'' Matthew said, and Lexy could breathe again. But he stopped suddenly and said, ''People change, Lexy. I've changed.''

She wanted to believe him, but fear gripped her heart and burned like acid on her tongue. ''No, you haven't, Matthew. You left Amanda. Just like you left me.''

Chapter Seventeen

Over the top of the magazine, Matthew watched Tasha help her grandmother pack the trunk. He'd sat in the living room for the past hour, pretending to read, but he couldn't concentrate. Not when Lexy had already packed her bags, which sat in the corner of his bedroom, taunting him, reminding him that after her family got on the plane tomorrow, she and Tasha would be moving back to her apartment.

One minute he was glad and looking forward to the peace and quiet, and not having to watch Lexy in his bed, knowing he couldn't touch her. The next minute he was ready to get on his knees and promise her anything to get them to stay.

He wouldn't do that, though. Not so much because of his pride, but because the next move had to be Lexy's. She had to want him in her life, like he wanted her. And Tasha. If he cornered her about Tasha now, Lexy might agree to make their marriage work only to avoid a custody battle. The thing was, he couldn't wait much longer.

He had never gone from angry to hurt and back to angry as much as he had in the past week.

Lexy should have told him about Tasha by now. He

had a right to know. He would never have guessed her to be the kind of woman who would deceive him that way. Of course, she didn't think much of the kind of man he was, he reminded himself. She'd loved him, and he'd left. Now he had to make her see that he'd changed.

He should have told her he loved her.

The curse that sprung to mind shouldn't have made it past his mouth, but when Tasha turned wide eyes on him, her lips starting to curve in a mischievous smile, he knew he'd slipped.

Smiling wryly at his daughter, he put a finger to his lips, asking her to keep their secret. She nodded and grinned, the tooth she'd lost just yesterday conspicuously absent.

Lexy was right to have hidden the truth. He was a bad father.

Sighing, he rubbed his eyes and sank deeper into the sofa cushions, watching the unsold inflatable lobsters get stored in the trunk. Lexy had gone to a lot of trouble to assure her family that she was okay here in America. She loved them and wanted to protect them, just like she loved and wanted to protect Tasha. Had she deceived him for reasons of greed or revenge, he wouldn't be able to forgive her. But Lexy had made her choice out of love.

Rationally he could tell himself this was true, but sometimes he still almost despised her for deceiving him, for depriving him of Tasha's first uttered word, her first step.

Life could have been easier for them both. He would have provided well for them, but Lexy had chosen to take the rough road rather than let him in. That stung the most.

Had she really thought so little of him as a man, as a potential father? Did she still? Was that why she'd rebuffed him that day at his parents' house?

He'd really screwed up over the weekend when he'd duped Lexy into going with him to see his family. He'd wanted her to meet them, see that they were good, moral, ordinary people who had raised him with solid values. She put a lot of stock in family, and he figured if she couldn't trust him, maybe she'd at least trust them enough to give him another chance.

But ever since their visit, Lexy had been subdued, distant. Of course, so had he. Seeing his family this time had been unsettling. In a good way. He had new respect for his father and how his father had made family his priority.

Maybe Lexy's conscience was getting to her. He hoped so. Maybe she'd finally trust him to do the right thing, trust that he wouldn't leave again. And not just because society wagged a finger at deadbeat dads. But because he loved her. He loved their daughter.

From the time he was a kid, Matt had craved power and respect, and with the success in his job, he'd achieved that and more. It was ironic that the one thing he'd ended up wanting most he couldn't have. More than ironic, it was damn poetic justice. Because he'd had Lexy's love and respect once and lost it.

He laughed, cursed under his breath, then shook his head.

Lost it, hell. He'd thrown it away. And now, all his money and power and obsessive self-importance couldn't get it back.

LEXY WAS TIDYING up when he entered the bedroom that night. Dinner had been a refined affair for the first time since the Constantines had descended upon his home. Everyone was sad over their departure tomorrow morning. Including Matt. Lexy would be returning to her apartment after their plane took off.

He looked at her packed bags stacked behind the door. He wished she wasn't so damned anxious.

"I didn't hear you," she said, glancing up and self-consciously tucking a stray tendril behind her ear.

He told himself to keep his hands to himself, then brushed a strand she'd missed off her cheek. Her skin was warm and soft and he forced himself to retreat.

She pressed her lips together and looked away. "I hope Dani doesn't stay out too late. Their flight leaves early," she said.

"Who is she with tonight, the cop or the grocery store guy?"

Lexy made a face. "Both. She couldn't decide."

Matt laughed, mostly because it was so good to see Lexy relaxed, looking like her old self. And because her sister was something else altogether. "And Serge? Did you give him a curfew?" he asked with a teasing grin.

Her smile promptly disappeared, replaced by a pained expression.

He understood the problem immediately and took her hand. "I know he's with Amanda. It's okay, Lexy," he said, ducking his head to meet her eyes. "Really. The wedding should have been called off long ago. It wasn't meant to be from the word go."

"Good." She blushed. "I mean, only because Amanda has plans to visit Serge next month."

"Hey, this could be serious. Maybe we'll have to team up again to attend *their* wedding."

She grinned, her eyes sparkling with pleasure. And

Matt chose to believe that the thought of their being together appealed to her.

Hope had his heart doing double time, and he realized his hold on her hand had tightened when she jerked. He brought her fingers to his lips, pressed a kiss to her palm. "Sorry, honey."

Her gaze lingered on his mouth, drifted to his eyes. He could kiss her and she wouldn't pull away. The timing probably wasn't right, there were too many emotional issues erecting a wall between them, but God help him, he couldn't resist.

And she didn't, either, when he lowered his lips to hers. Instead she clung to him with bittersweet abandon, her arms slipping around his neck, pulling him closer.

Despite her apparent willingness, he didn't want to scare her off, and kept the kiss from getting too hungry. But his good intentions lasted only a fleeting moment when Lexy pressed her body to his, her breasts rubbing him, causing a friction against his chest he could barely stand. He slid a hand between them to cup her fullness. And they were full, fuller than they had been seven years ago. Probably because of Tasha.

Their daughter.

He pulled back slightly and framed her face with his hands. "Ah, Lexy." He wanted her to tell him about Tasha so much it hurt. But he wouldn't pry it out of her. He'd wait. It had to be that way. "I want you, Lexy," he said, a smile starting to curve one side of his mouth, his desire taking on a life of its own. "But I guess that's no secret."

She gave him a shy smile, her lashes fluttering.

"You know, we *are* still legally married," he said, wondering what the hell was wrong with him.

Making love at this point would complicate things. Sex right now would be a weapon. Except he wasn't using sex and he certainly wasn't using Lexy. He loved her. He just couldn't tell her yet.

"True," she whispered, and whether consciously or not, she shimmied against him, diminishing all reason into a cascade of hopeless longing pooling in his groin.

Without another damning thought, he slipped his arms beneath her, lifted her feet off the carpet, then laid her on the bed.

She whimpered in surprise but eagerly returned her arms to their rightful place around his neck.

"Be okay with this, Lexy," he whispered before pressing a kiss to her throat, trailing it up to her jaw, her ear, her lips.

She didn't respond with words. She arched her back off the mattress to make contact with him. Her small, perfect breasts thrust into the air, and with a shaky hand he cupped one.

Two buttons of her blouse had already come undone, and in seconds he freed the rest. The front clasp of her bra took a mere flick, and then her beautiful, unbound breasts stole his breath. Her nipples had already blossomed before his tongue touched their rosy sweetness, and he wasn't sure how long he could restrain himself.

Lexy's impatience took care of that dilemma. She clawed at his shirt until she'd yanked it off his head, jerked on his zipper until he feared she'd hurt something vital. In both their interests, he helped her out, getting rid of her shorts and panties at the same time.

She lay back against the cream-colored pillows, her face and body slightly flushed from their fevered efforts. She was so damn beautiful she made his chest ache.

He bowed his head to taste her breasts again, but she cupped his cheek and brought his face up so that their gazes met. She bit her lip in a touchingly shy gesture but her darkened brown eyes looked determined. "I want you inside me, Matthew."

He took a quick breath, gave a slow, satisfied smile as he positioned himself above her, then slid home.

Lexy sighed and moaned as she cradled his hips with her thighs. She whispered his name, clawed at his back, met each thrust with enthusiasm. But when they finally exploded in each other's arms, their hearts pounding the same rhythm, she still hadn't said she loved him.

He kissed the damp skin near her temple, tightened his hold around her waist as he rolled off, hoping she'd go with him so that he could keep her snuggled against his chest. Even more, Matt hoped this was a new beginning.

But when Lexy broke away and hurried toward the bathroom, ignoring his plea for her to come back, it felt depressingly like goodbye.

THROUGH A FRESH round of tears, Lexy listened to the last boarding call, then gave her father a final hug. Her sister was weeping dramatically, earning her the attention of every male from three gates. Lexy gave her a watery smile before turning to her mother.

"Travel safe," she said in Hungarian, and wrapped her arms around her warm, familiar body. "I love you."

Her mother sniffled as she pulled back to look at Lexy. She squeezed her daughter's hands, then pressed them to her cheeks. "You make me so proud," she whispered. "Don't be foolish, child."

Lexy blinked at the unexpected words, then watched with dread as her mother lowered her hands and turned up her palms.

"You love him, but you have too much fear in your heart," she said, studying the creases in Lexy's skin. "This fear is wrong. It will hurt you if you don't let love in."

Although her mother did not know the entire story, she'd guessed there was a problem, and had pulled Lexy aside yesterday for a heart-to-heart. To her relief, her mom thought it best to keep the matter between them. That's how sure she was everything would work out. Lexy let her have her false hope.

"You must go now," Lexy said, withdrawing her hands and kissing her mother's cheek again. "They are closing the door."

Her mother gave her a final hug and hurried toward the jetway where the rest of the family beckoned her. Tasha had stayed glued to Matthew's side through all the hugging and kissing, and even now she clung to him as they all waved until the entire Constantine clan was out of sight.

"Are you okay?" Matt asked her, concern in his voice as he tried to slip an arm around her shoulders.

She nodded, ducking away from him, though not in an obvious way, and bent to give Tasha a hug. "Did you have fun, honey?"

"Yes," she said, then yawned and took Lexy's hand. The other one she placed firmly in Matthew's. He smiled down at her.

Lexy tried not to notice, she tried not to think about the damage she may have caused. Within the hour,

Matthew would be out of Tasha's life forever. Out of hers.

Or maybe now that Amanda was out of the way...

This wasn't about Amanda, Lexy reminded herself. Lexy had deceived Matthew, and when she finally admitted it, he wouldn't want her. And yet she was sure he already knew....

Lexy swallowed and ended up hiccuping. This was so confusing. Especially when she was tired from so little sleep. She need only remember that nothing had changed.

Not even their lovemaking last night had altered their course. Matthew wanted different things in life, which did not include a family. It was so obvious Tasha was his daughter. Lexy believed with all her heart Matthew knew that her dear, sweet child was his, yet he remained steadfastly silent. That should be proof enough for her stubborn heart.

But she still loved him, anyway, and it hurt. With the three of them walking hand in hand toward the car, it hurt even more than she thought possible.

The ride home was long and silent, until they reached Matthew's house and Tasha realized they wouldn't be staying. She sniffled and whined the entire time he soberly carried their bags to the car, then she began to sob in earnest when they pulled up in front of the apartment and Matthew carried in their bags.

Lexy tried to calm her before getting out of the car, but Tasha refused to listen.

Upon his return, Matthew immediately lifted her into his arms. "Hey," he said, tweaking her nose. "What're the tears for?"

"I don't like it here anymore," she said, struggling for a breath and breaking Lexy's heart.

"Ah, and here I thought you were going to miss me."

A brief smile touched Tasha's lips before they jutted out in a pout. "I wish you were my father."

Lexy choked back a sob.

Matthew paled and gave Tasha a weak smile. "I'll see you again soon, okay?"

"When?"

Panic swept Lexy. She didn't want Matthew to feel cornered, and she didn't want him making her daughter promises he couldn't keep. "Come on," she said, reaching for Tasha. "Matthew has things to do."

"Not Matthew, it's Popo," Tasha said, her face scrunching up in a frown. "Right?"

"Right," he confirmed, his expressionless eyes meeting Lexy's as she took Tasha away from him.

"Thank you, Matthew," Lexy said, setting Tasha down beside her on the sidewalk. Her little girl was getting heavy. She was growing up so fast.

And Matthew had missed out on all of it.

Lexy's breath caught. She had to get upstairs. She needed privacy. She needed to get away from Matthew.

"Come on, Tasha." Glancing at him, she said, "I'll talk to you later, huh?"

"Sure." He shrugged. "I've got to go, anyway. I have this high-profile case tomorrow...."

Of course he did, she thought, and rushed through the doors of her apartment building before he'd even finished speaking. Work was everything to Matthew.

"Mommy, I didn't get to say goodbye to Popo," Tasha complained loudly, and when Lexy ignored her, she whined all the way up the stairs.

She was still fussing as Lexy fumbled with the lock,

prompting Mrs. Hershey to peek out her door. "Land sakes, I'm happy to see you two. It's been lonely and quiet around here."

As difficult as she found the simple gesture, Lexy returned the woman's smile. It wasn't Mrs. Hershey's fault that Lexy was falling apart, that her heart was shattering in her chest. The woman had been nothing but kind to her and Tasha and she deserved more than a brush-off.

Even Tasha stopped whining long enough to give their neighbor a big grin. "Look, Mrs. Hershey, I lost a tooth."

"Oh, my." The older woman stepped into the corridor, clutching a hand to her chest. "Did the tooth fairy visit you?"

Tasha nodded. "She left me five dollars."

Mrs. Hershey's eyes widened, then she briefly glanced at Lexy. "Well, isn't that wonderful?"

Lexy pushed open the door. "Tasha, go get washed up and I'll be right in to make lunch."

"Okay." She sighed dramatically, sounding much like Dani as she stomped inside. "But I wish Popo was eating with us."

Mrs. Hershey chuckled as soon as Tasha was out of earshot. "Let me guess who slipped her the five dollars."

Lexy sighed even louder than her daughter. "I tried to tell him that was too much." She waved a hand, not wanting to discuss Matthew in any way. What she needed was to *not* think about him. Because if she did...

"What's the matter? You look so pale all of a sudden." Mrs. Hershey patted her shoulder. "Your parents just left, didn't they?"

"Yes," Lexy said hurriedly, anxious to lock herself in the bathroom. "Maybe I could make us some tea later?"

The older woman nodded her understanding. "I know you must be tired, but your grades came yesterday. You've been anxious for them and your mailbox was full, so Gilbert left it with me. Shall I bring the envelope over later or do you want it now?"

A startled gasp escaped Lexy's lips. She'd totally forgotten about her grades. How could she have?

"Do you need to sit down, dear?"

"No, no, I'm fine." She took a deep breath. "I, uh, I'll just get it now," she said, and walked past Mrs. Hershey when the woman hesitated, her anxious gaze studying Lexy's face.

She stopped outside the door and waited for her neighbor to go into her apartment first, then followed her to the kitchen.

Mrs. Hershey picked an envelope up off the counter and handed it to her, her probing gaze never leaving Lexy's face. "It's Matthew, isn't it?"

Lexy shook her head at first, then nodded. "But he's left, and it's over."

Confusion drew the woman's gray brows together. "He left because it's over?"

"Matthew always leaves, Mrs. Hershey." A breath caught in Lexy's throat. She had to get out of here before she broke down in front of the poor woman and scared her to death. Lexy was headed for a good earth-rocking cry and she wasn't sure she'd be able to stop it. "He just always does."

Mrs. Hershey's kind eyes softened, and her mouth curved in a gentle smile. "Seems to me he was always rushing in, not leaving."

Lexy blinked. It wasn't that simple. Matthew had come to her rescue only because she'd practically blackmailed him. And then...

And then he'd just kept coming, even when she hadn't asked for his help.

She was getting awfully confused again. Maybe he *had* changed. Maybe she was too big a coward to confess her own deceit.

She sniffed. "Thanks for keeping my mail," she said on her way out. "I'll call you later after we've both had naps."

She rushed across the hall into her drab apartment, closed her door and sank against it. Taking a moment to pull herself together, she dabbed at her eyes, swiped the moisture from her cheek. It wasn't as if she was never going to see him again. After all, she still had to sign the divorce papers.

The thought didn't cheer her, and she took a deep breath as she pushed away from the door and called for Tasha.

No answer.

"Tasha? Have you washed up?" she called again.

The apartment was deafeningly silent.

"Tasha." Lexy ran to the bathroom, found nothing, and ran to the bedroom. "Tasha," she shouted again, even though it was obvious the apartment was empty.

Oh, my, God. Her heart dipped with sickening speed.

Lexy dashed to Mrs. Hershey's door and pounded on it, knowing it was impossible for her daughter to have gotten past her. As soon as the other woman opened the door with a surprised look, Lexy crumpled.

"Tasha isn't in the apartment," she said, her voice barely working.

"Maybe she forgot something outside?"

Lexy took several quick, shallow breaths, trying to calm down. That was it. Tasha had left something on the sidewalk. Without saying another word to Mrs. Hershey, she ran for the stairs, taking them two at a time all the way down.

Except for three little girls jumping rope nearly a block away, the sidewalk was empty.

Lexy covered her mouth with a trembling hand. *Matthew*. Maybe Tasha had...

She ran back up the stairs and dug through her purse for the cell phone she'd forgotten to return to him. After two failed attempts, she punched in Matthew's car phone number.

"HAVE YOU CALLED the police?" Matthew asked as he rushed through the door ten minutes later. His hair was a wreck, his face drawn and pale. "Call the police now. Dial 911. Tell them she may have been kidnapped." He stopped, a stricken expression clouding his features as he took Lexy's hand. "I don't think she was. I just want to get them moving."

Lexy flung herself at him. "This is all my fault."

"Of course it isn't," he said, holding her close. "She's just wandered off," he said, brushing the hair away from her eyes. "We're going to find her, and then we're going to ground her for a month. Maybe even until she's thirty."

"But she's never done this before." Tears streamed down Lexy's cheeks. What had she done? She had to tell Matthew the truth. And Tasha, too.

His eyes were glassy, dark, troubled. He looked awful. And then he smiled...a smile meant to reassure her. "She disappeared the first day she met your parents, remember? We found her then and we'll find her now. Have you checked with the neighbors?''

She nodded, then shook her head. ''One of them. Mrs. Hershey is checking with the others now. I'm supposed to stay by the phone.'' He was right. Tasha *had* done this before, two weeks ago. And just as he'd done now, Matthew had run to the rescue. He was right about something else, too. They were going to find Tasha. And she would be safe. Lexy knew it in her heart.

She sniffed, hiccuped. Mrs. Hershey was also right. It suddenly seemed like everyone was right but Lexy. The old Matthew had changed, and the new one was always there when she needed him. Even when she'd thrown his support back in his face, he hadn't wavered once. So why hadn't he acknowledged Tasha?

It didn't matter. She could no longer justify withholding the truth. Not that she'd ever had the right. But to continue to do so would eat her alive. ''I have something to tell you.''

His gaze turned wary, then he gave her a tentative smile and squeezed her shoulder. ''Let's find Tasha first, okay?''

''No.'' She pushed away from him, sending up a little prayer that the words wouldn't get tangled up in her mouth. She had a lot to tell him, none of it easy. But Lexy could no longer deny that Matthew had changed. He'd grown up. It was time she did, too. ''What I have to tell you is about Tasha.''

''Lexy, this can wait.''

''It can't.'' Her voice cracked. She was still being a coward, she realized. She wanted to tell him now, when they wouldn't have time to hash things out.

There would be time for that later. If he was still

speaking to her. Taking a deep breath and closing her eyes, she said, "Tasha is your daughter."

Her announcement was met with complete silence, and when she peeked through her lashes at him, he looked solemn but not too horribly angry. She wished he'd say something. Anything.

"Matthew?" A lump blocked her throat, making the words hard to form. Maybe she'd been wrong telling him now. It seems she'd been wrong about many things. "We don't both need to wait by the phone. If you stay here, I'll—"

A noise came from the bedroom. It sounded like a loud yawn. Lexy might have thought she'd imagined it, except Matthew glanced curiously in that direction, too.

She rushed down the short hall with him right behind her.

Just as they got to the bedroom door, Tasha rolled out from under the bed. She immediately got to her feet and gave them a gap-toothed grin. "I knew I heard you, Popo."

"Tasha!" Lexy rushed in and gathered her daughter's small body in her arms. "We were so worried about you."

"I was right here, Mom, taking a nap."

Lexy pulled back to give her a firm look. "*Under* the bed?"

Tasha gave a mischeivous smile as she glanced at Matthew. "I knew Popo would come back," she whispered.

Lexy's entire body tightened and she couldn't stop the tears that erupted. Even her daughter had figured out the truth Lexy had been too fearful, too stubborn to see.

How could she have been so blind? She and Matthew, they weren't that different, she'd realized as she waited for him. He'd been up front about the security and material comforts he wanted. *She'd* been the dishonest one. She'd lied to her parents about all the things she didn't have. And in her deceit, she'd hurt the people she cared about most.

Matthew must have seen the irony, yet he'd said nothing. She was so ashamed. She didn't even want to look at him.

"Tasha," Matthew said from behind them, his voice stern. "I'm glad you're okay, but you were very wrong to scare your mother and me like that. Do you understand?"

Tasha's eyes grew large as she nodded. She looked to Lexy for help. Lexy said nothing. Matthew was right and she wouldn't interfere.

"I'm sorry," Tasha said, staring down at her toes. "I didn't mean to worry anyone. I just wanted us to be a family again."

Lexy hadn't thought her heart could break any more. She slid a reluctant look at Matthew.

He was smiling.

"Me, too," he said, and opened his arms.

Tasha eagerly went to him, and Lexy already could feel her daughter slipping away. It would never be just the two of them again. Her father would now be a part of her life. Just as he should be. Lexy bowed her head. It was just so hard to think about...

"Lexy?"

She looked up.

Matthew had scooped Tasha up and held her to him with one arm. He held his other hand out to Lexy.

Her heart pounding, her eyes met Tasha's happy

ones. Was this show for Tasha's sake? Or did Matthew still think they had a chance?

She laid her palm in his, and as he pulled her to her feet, their gazes locked. Something she dared to believe was love flared in his eyes before he turned to smile at their daughter, his hand still firmly holding Lexy's.

"Tasha? How would you like it if I were your daddy?"

She grinned and threw her arms around his neck. "Can we live at your house?"

He laughed, staggering slightly under her enthusiasm, then looked at Lexy again. "We have a lot to discuss."

She nodded, miserable...hopeful...afraid. "I know you're angry," she whispered, and her hand automatically went out to stroke the back of Tasha's head, the gesture comforting her more than her daughter.

Matthew stepped back, taking Tasha out of Lexy's reach, and her heart plummeted to her stomach. He set their daughter on the floor. "Princess, why don't you go to the kitchen and have a snack?"

"And then can we go back to your house?"

His eyes met Lexy's. "I don't see why not. Do you?"

Everything was going to work out, Lexy thought, her pulse racing. She heard it in his voice, saw the promise in his eyes. She couldn't speak, though, and blessed Tasha for scampering off to the kitchen.

"The truth?" Matthew said as soon as Tasha was out of earshot. "Yeah, I'm a little angry. And we have some issues to get out of the way. But I love you, Lexy," he said, moving closer and taking hold of her arms. "And nothing is going to change that."

"I love you, too," she said in a small voice. "I've always loved you, Matthew."

His eyes got a little glassy as he pulled her against him and rested his chin on the top of her head. "You've done a great job with her, honey."

Lexy sniffed. "I'm so sorry, Matthew."

"Hush," he whispered, putting her slightly away from him so he could look at her. He bent down and brushed her lips with his. "I have a lot to be sorry for, too. More than I can explain. But we have even more to be grateful for. We have a second chance, Lexy. How many people get that in life?"

She nodded, the numbness wearing off and happiness filling her. "I do love you so much, Matthew."

"I love you." Framing her face with his hands, he lowered his face to hers.

"I'm ready. Can we go now?"

Matthew smiled at Lexy before he straightened, and they both turned to look at Tasha. She'd tied a yellow ribbon around one pigtail, a pink one around the other. On top of her head sat a small blue bow.

He laughed. "She may be my daughter, but she definitely takes after your side of the family."

If you enjoyed what you just read,
then we've got an offer you can't resist!

Take 2 bestselling
love stories FREE!
Plus get a FREE surprise gift!

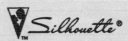

COMING NEXT MONTH

#793 WILDCAT COWBOY by Cathy Gillen Thacker
The McCabes of Texas
Wade McCabe was not a Texan to be messed with. Only, nobody told that to Josie Corbett, who was every bit his equal. And while Josie wasn't looking to play a role in any McCabe baby-making scheme, she did want to lasso wildcat Wade on her own terms. But there was no resisting this Texas playboy—or his matchmaking family.

#794 BABY BY MIDNIGHT? by Karen Toller Whittenburg
Delivery Room Dads
Alex McIntyre knew Annie Thatcher was pregnant with *his* baby—but the stubborn woman wouldn't admit it! Alex hadn't forgotten their steamy night of passion—no way was Annie going to the delivery room alone when Alex was right there, finally ready to be a husband and daddy!

#795 THE VIRGIN & HER BODYGUARD by Mindy Neff
Tall, Dark & Irresistible
Raquel Santiago's small country home was not big enough for her, her baby photography studio and one very brawny man. Babies to the left, babies to the right and Cole Martinez covered in infant spit-up and all-male sweat. He radiated strength and virility and gentleness that Raquel could not resist. Cole was all too happy to indulge her fantasies—except for his promise to her father....

#796 A MATCH MADE IN TEXAS by Tina Leonard
For a woman who had never known romance, Mary van Doorn was getting a double helping from Jake Maddox. But with the responsibility of six sisters and their sunflower farm, she was *not* shopping for a man. The locals, though, had a different plan: one that would keep the population of small-town Sunflower Junction, Texas, on the rise!

Look us up on-line at: http://www.romance.net